CW00519383

IN PRINT

Stories that Belong

CM
Scotts

Vol. 2

In Print – The stories that belong

© Copyright 2017 CM Scotts

All Rights Reserved. This publication is provided subject to the condition that it shall not, by way of trade or otherwise, be lent, resold, hired out or otherwise circulated without the author's prior written consent. No part of this book may be reproduced by any process including electronic, mechanical, photocopying, recording or otherwise, without the prior written permission of the author. Nor may it be stored in a retrieval system, transmitted or otherwise copied for public or private use without the written permission of the author. Any trademarks, service marks, product names or named features are the property of their respective owners. There is no implied endorsement for the usage of these terms.

This book is dedicated to the proprietors of the world.
Those humans who share their customs,
their tables and their fire. Gracias por todo.

Acknowledgements

To Roel and Anja. The Dutch couple who taught me how to roll and offered me a place on the other side of the Atlantic.

To Bruno. To the lonely man from Belgium. "To fall in love is the easy, to fall from love is the pain."

Contents

To travel is to discover that everyone is wrong about other countries.

— Aldous Huxley

Chapter 1

The hook

Eustace dreamed of her again, he always dreamed of her now.

Usually when he awoke, the dreams would fleet away. One by one the dreamspace memory would fade with the intrusion of daylight. When he sat up in his humble bed he looked at the rosary and the crucifix that hung from the wall. The Christ figure hung bloodied and lifeless. Eustace reached out, yearning for someone to embrace. With no one to return the yearn, he stood naked in his room. This morning, like every morning, he clasped his hands and prayed.

Through the dark wooden slats the morning sun was blinding. Eustace sat himself on the small wooden chair and lowered his head into his hands. He did not want to pray anymore. He didn't want to be servant of God anymore, he wanted to be a fisherman. A great fisherman with a salted beard and weathered hands.

Ocean breezes and beach side parasols sounded ideal. The capital city of Cardiff was cold, Eustace was cold. The warmth and security of the white collar no longer soothed him.

He took a long look at the grandfather clock. It read 6.17 am. His sermon was set to being in one hour. Three books lay face up on his humble breakfast table. The Holy Bible, Moby Dick and the missionary guide to Central America. Eustace had always been interested in the warm lands of the Americas. He sat in the darkened parish room and decided he would give his daily sermon to the squalid lot that were his sheep. Then he would talk to the Bishop.

"One last time." He said to himself.

After his sermon and after a guilt laden lecture from the Bishop, Eustace returned to the Brothel to see the only woman he ever held feelings for. Her name was Fernande, the proprietor of "Sugars". Most often she would comfort him by simply allowing him to read to her. She was most often drunk, but she did enjoy the stories.

She laughed and giggled when the man with the collar would sit in her house of ill refute.

Not once did they engage in sexual relations. At most, she would lay her legs across his lap while he read. Sometimes she would kiss his forehead before retiring to her elegant chamber alone.

In Print

On this day, he came to her with the last chapter. She sipped her wine and smoked her expensive tobacco as he entered.

After he read to the madam for the last time the fire lost heat and the glow of the embers faded into the mantel of ashes. Fernande lay asleep under the bear skin rug as she often did.

When Eustace finished the book he stood quietly and penned a note.

"One day, we shall meet again."

-Ahab

● ● ●

Two days later.

As Eustace stood on the splintered bow of Sala de Sala his stomach felt empty.

To his surprise and delight he saw Fernande on the shore. She was walking towards him, down the pier in her favorite red dress. A large feathered hat sat upon her brow. She walked to the very edge, took a deep breath then kissed her hands.

For the first time in her life she said goodbye to a man she would truly miss. Fernande threw him a kiss with both hands then made a heart shape with her fingers. She placed the shape above her own beating heart then waved a long arm farewell.

Eustace reached out to catch the kiss. He had never felt love before, and he held little hope for the lost sheep of his world. But not this sheep. Something about this sheep would remain unforgettable. He did not send a heart shape back. He simply stood at the stern of the boat as the final ropes were freed from the dock.

That day Eustace left the Brothel, the Church and the only woman he ever wanted to kiss.

Two days into the journey he met a Dutchman named Topo.

That night she sat alone in her room. The front door was locked, there would be no solicitors. Fernande sadly and slowly tossed the drawing she made of Eustace into the smoldering fire.

Chapter 2

En este libro

I am traveling to South America to meet with Troy Hibbons. Troy was running amuck and I needed a change of pace. The plan was to meet in Buenos Aires, climb through the Andes, then relax on an island. I was en route from Mexico and weary of trains, exhausted by nothing more than the lugging and chugging vibrations of the steel wheels.

I fear that I will not have the ability to portray for you this person. This person that is Troy. But I will do my best as I was commissioned to do so by a handshake on the beach. If I learned anything from Troy, it was that "a handshake is a real thing" and

"Life. A journey of lights, colors, and sounds."

Over a few years Troy and I collected 42 passport stamps and more stories than I can recall. To this day I still recite idioms and inside jokes with a dead man. Troy was an artist.

He could draw anything with a piece of lead or a blade of grass.

Before he died he left me a large pile of his poetry and his sketches. So, for the love of my dear friend Troy, I will do my best to tell the stories. Troy taught me how to travel. He taught me how to stay light on my feet and how to indulge in the offerings of life, whether they be good or bad.

He would often sneak out in the night and leave me a note with some vague directions. In time, I would do the same for him. Troy is the man who taught me how to live scot-free.

We loved each other like brothers. We took care of each other when the other faltered, but somehow, we didn't have much in common. He lived a life of unabashed freedom and was somehow incredibly capable of fleeting danger. By the seat of his pants he traveled most of the world. Troy, tetched only by the wars of the world and the sheer injustice of it all, held no grudges against any one person in particular. I could not say those things for myself.

Chapter 3

Guillaume

Six days and 7000 miles later I moved into a small Argentinian hostel. It was a small private room with a shared kitchen and a parking lot view. Groggy from the bus but eager to settle in, I unpacked the few clothes I had.

For the length of the journey, my mind reeled with memories from my recent dreams and the stories I heard along the way. I was now on the far side of the planet. No longer surrounded by lush green fields and old dirt roads, I was in Buenos Aires, and a storm was brewing.

From my tiny room I could hear the thunder and lightning strike together.

A flickering of skyward lights provoked an immediate deluge. I laid upon my new little bed with the window open. The rain spattered on the sill and hammered down like a thousand turrets on my rooftop.

Satisfied by the performance, I stepped outside to find my flatmate, Guillaume. A French bioengineering researcher on loan from the Universite Paris. The assistant professor was long and lean with hollow blue eyes. He rolled smokes with pleasure and sipped pressed coffee with pursed lips. The two of us stood under the thin metal awning and listened to the orchestra pound. We shook hands and greeted each other cordially.

"Americano?" he said with his cigarette in his lips.

"Yea, what of it?" I bristled. He chuckled.

"Aye, you are Americano. Would you like?"

"What?"

"Possibly, a flat white?"

"What are you talking about?"

He was smiling, and I figured he was making fun. He continued to look with amusement. I finally noticed his empty café glass and smashed cigarette.

"Oh. Would I like a coffee?...No, thanks."

He laughed then flung the screen door open to proceed inside. Standing on the porch of my new little abode I stepped out onto the grass and let the rain pound upon my shoulders. The lightning storm was incredible.

The next morning a knock on my door produced the very tall Guillaume.

"Good morning. You are new here, yes? I am going to the beach for a book, would you like to accompany? It is quite far."

"Sure," I said.

"I will pick you in 10 minutes, yes?"

"Sure."

Exactly 10 minutes later he returned. It was no Sunday stroll; we were headed for Silver Beach. First we walked through a busy parking lot. Then, without talking, we walked a half mile through the gray and uninteresting parts of the city. All cities have them. It is the part of the city forgotten in gray bricks and potholed streets.

Finally, near Puerto Madero we jumped a chain-link fence. Then we jogged across a futbol field and over a highway bridge. Finally we stepped onto a small train platform at the edge of the suburbs. Guillaume was kind enough to buy my first train ticket. I stood on the platform completely blind to our destination. Once the train arrived we boarded and found a comfortable chair with a view.

The train didn't chug forward as I expected. It was an electric train, and quite new. The same unsettling and exciting feeling I had in the airport happened again. It was a welling of heat and nervousness in my lower belly. The sensation wasn't alarming or traumatic, it was just, there. The strange feeling faded once the train hummed to full speed.

After thirty-two minutes and seven stops, we stepped off the train as the loud speaker repeated,

"Menta la brecha. Menta la brecha."

From the platform a big blue sign read, "Playa," with an arrow pointing east. We followed the shore birds and the flock of suntanned blancos straight to a bus stop. Standing at the bus stop, Guillame smoked while I gawked at the city center. It was a huge square with thousands of human heads painted on the stone tiles. Empanada and maté vendors stood everywhere. Even though I was on the other side of the planet, I knew the smell of sunblock and sandy, gritty floors. The beach was close. Guillaume grabbed me by the arm and pulled me across the street.

"The bus is leave now."

We jumped on and again Guillaume paid my fare. When we finally arrived at the beach I was astonished. There it was: a beautiful blue Atlantic ocean. The waves were tall and curling. The sun was blaring down and everyone looked happy. Locals and tourists alike hunkered under giant umbrellas. They paid no attention to the dozens of children running around. Boys and girls of all colors and clothing happily threw plastic toys and kicked at their sand castles.

Guillaume placed a hand on my shoulder and pointed toward the large red plastic chicken on the roof of a food stand, it was a fast food chain selling a fried chicken sandwich doused in warm mayonnaise. Then he pointed out the bus stop signs. Guillaume walked into the nearest bookstore. I'm not sure why, but I tried one of the fried chicken sandwiches. Hot mayonnaise on a hot day turned my stomach sideways. The slippery bread pooled chicken grease below my tongue. The meal was unsatisfying and left me with a thirst for...something. I couldn't place what.

Beer, I thought. That's the ticket.

I couldn't find a book I wanted, nor did I have any of the items one needs for the beach. I told Guillaume I would find him later. He agreed with a glance and I left to find a cold one. Luckily, the local merchants like beer as well, especially on a hot day. There were several places to grab a bite to eat and something to drink in Mar de Plata.

An hour passed. By now Guillaume was growing anxious to leave the beach as we still had a long journey back to Buenos Aires. The beer was six dollars and a gold coin. I paid it and it did indeed settle my stomach. After I wandered my way down to the bus stop I found Guillaume perfectly poised on the concrete steps. From there he could read his new book, *Italian 101*, while eyeing a beautiful Argentine woman. She lay on her back topless and completely shaded under a yellow parasol. As I approached him he closed his book and stood tall.

"We go. Is important." Guillaume and I were now on an impromptu hunt for a woman named Sira. She was an Italian with…"French, beautiful, perfect hair, and eyes of emeralds." Guillame described her as pure gold.

She worked as a waitress at one of the small restaurants in an area called "el bloc." Old stone buildings lined the steep and narrow streets. Each of the buildings shared a narrow alley complete with homeless dogs and graffiti. Each entryway announced the family colors in bright paint. It was a part of Buenos Aires that felt very old. I wanted to stay longer but I was swept up into whatever Guillame had planned for this lady.

"Come with me," he said at a quick pace. "You will know Sira. She will be in the eyes of everyone in the room."

"Ok," I said, moving through pedestrians to keep pace.

We walked a few short blocks through an artsy tourist trap until we came upon "La Sabora," a café offering empanadas, crepes, and coffee, according to the window. He smiled and we entered. Guillaume was right. There was a woman working in that small restaurant and she held everyone's attention. Her curves and curls accentuated a long black dress and a ruby pendant. We were seated at a small table by the host. When we sat, Guillame prepared to order for us.

Sira noticed Guillame. Soon she floated to our table. She stood tall for the average woman, and her cinnamon skin was radiant, polished by the sun. Faint eyebrows and powerful dark green eyes matched her reddish brunette curls. Guillame looked her square in the eyes and ordered in Italian.

As she began to write the order, she softly hummed the words to the song overhead. She then placed her hand on my shoulder, nonchalant. Guillaume continued speaking to her in Italian. He labored, but Sira understood. She began to blush. Guillaume winked and then said with a grin,

"Vai, avanti."

Our crepes showed up soon after and strangely Sira wrote us two tickets. One with the bill and the other with an XO on it. I sat in astonishment as Guillaume ate exactly half of his crepe, all the while grinning like an idiot. I didn't eat much of mine, as I had developed an excruciating headache. Sira continued to mesmerize the floor with her Italian flare as we ate. On the walk back I asked Guillaume, "Why two?"

He smiled.

"It is her test of me." He withdrew the card from his inner pocket.

"Smell it. It smells of her perfume." We stopped at the train tracks under a streetlamp. I smelled it, then I looked at him flat.

"Americans lack subtlety. I must know her scent if I am to dance with her again. This is truth," he said while holding the card in front of his face.

"But, you didn't dance with her."

He pointed two fingers at my face.

"The dance always begin in the eye. Tonight we danced. This woman is passion. This woman smells of romance." He took a long smell of the card then gently placed it into his shirt pocket.

We walked through the crowd of summer tourists and boarded the train. My headache hadn't subsided and Guillaume wasn't much for conversation. He sat with his eyes closed the entire train ride. Once we departed the train we still had an hour walk back to the hostel. My skin felt as rough as sandpaper and my tongue was swollen inside my mouth.

When Guillame and I walked through the plaza, a few of our new neighbors were sitting around the café bar. They invited us to join them, which at the time seemed harmless. After a few bottles went around the table my head began to spin and my back ached with a pulsating throb. Delirious and dizzy, I excused myself from the table and stumbled down the stone path. Looking up at the Argentine night sky, I tripped on the steps and left a face print on my front door. Nevertheless, I made into my tiny room and collapsed onto my very own little concrete floor.

Guillame and I spent a few days together and, as I grew to learn, the best friendships often last but a few days. He and I shared a café Americano in recognition of our first date. He looked across the small table and added, while rolling an aperitif, "There are many angels here. Perhaps you can find one."

"Perhaps I will, Guillame. Perhaps I will."

We wished each other well and I struck off down the road and back into the city. I was traveling light and life seemed to be shining. While riding the train I couldn't help but think of life back home. There wasn't anything to miss, a one horse town with a bar and a post office. I wondered what happened to Mari, and Doc and Jack. I wondered and hoped James was running free somewhere in the far far meadows.

"I'm sure they're fine," I said to myself.

Chapter 4

Sticky icky

The next day I wandered through the metropolis for several hours. Flocks of pigeons ran like beetles toward the seagulls in the street near Casa Rosado. The birds were fighting over a large basket of bread that fell off a small motorbike. The delivery boy saw the basket fall but he didn't return for it. Soon several big pink feathers and soft gray bellies were posturing like a gang of rebels. The two groups would run at each other then fly a short distance into the air. As each bird squawked as it would land back within its group. One of the seagulls walked into the middle of the road but stopped short of the pigeons. I laughed at them and imagined the little bully pigeons with Coastie accents.

I must have stared at the pigeons for some time. Two different Argentines stopped on the sidewalk to ask if I was all right. Both of them placed a hand on my shoulder and looked concerned.

"Todo bien?" they asked.

"Todo, bien," I told them both. "Mirando a los pajaros. Payasos."

With little concern, the locals shook their heads and continued on their way. Now standing near the centro intersection I heard something familiar.

Phiiiit.

A shrill whistle from across the square could only have come from one person. Troy Hibbons. There he stood, two meters of Vancouver Canadian long haired blond. A man set on devouring life and barreling through the world's offerings was waving at me with both arms.

Phiiit.

He whistled again. I ran toward him and crossed the street with haste.

"Hey mate, what's up? I was on my way to your hostel."

"Oh yea, good. Me too. What's been happening?"

"Nada mucho...I've been hanging out, skipping around the planet, you know. What about you, white blood? You hittin' it hard or what?"

"I've been working too much," I said with a quick breath.

18

In Print

"Well. We'll see we put an end to that. Come with me, your new place is this way." He marched off across the street and I turned to follow.

"Yours is the one with the big orange wall, right?"

"Yea."

"Aight. We're gone. Jump to a midlane." Troy began barking directions at me as we picked through traffic.

"You look thirsty." A bus ground by. "And you're sunburnt. WOULD!" he shouted while jutting an arm straight up to the heavens. "Tonight is jeans night. Make sure you shower and nap. Go. Go!"

I trusted him and jumped into traffic. Surprisingly, I skipped right through the lanes, unscathed. On the other side he stood tall with his hands on his hips.

"Dinner starts at 10."

From here, Troy and I employed a smooth pace as we walked a kilometer or so deeper into the city.

There it was, my hostel. The one with the big orange wall. In downtown Buenos Aires there are several hostels. Argentines have good taste. My hostel in the big pink building was near the tourist district of Puerto Madero. A small metal gate between two concrete walls opens up to a dirt path. That dirt path leads to a tiny little paradise. That tiny little forested alley led to a wooden desk. That desk led to a flat faced man named Carlos.

Carlos was the gatekeeper. His slacks appeared uncomfortable and tight, and the buttons on his light blue shirt strained against his belly.

"This is the guy I told you about," Troy said to Carlos.

Carlos shook my hand then rummaged around in a little black metal box that sat on the wooden desk. He looked up at me and handed me two keys and a small piece of paper.

"Bienvenido," he said. Then he sat back down in his chair and opened the white wooden door to his left. It led to a small café with croissants, coffee, and several metal chairs.

One large pink parasol covered the ground with a mesmerizing hue. Troy slapped me on the back.

"Let's eat," he said.

A few little tables with chairs for no more than two sat under the nearest umbrella. A square staircase rose in the middle of the courtyard. It is painted egg white and blaze orange. It leads four stories up, and each level you pass hosts a row of dorm rooms.

"This hostel used to be someone's house," Troy said with croissant in his teeth. "It has a feel of a neutral place and the master bedrooms are on the top deck."

"How do you know that?"

"Oh, I met a Chilean girl a few months back. We stayed up stairs." He pointed two fingers straight up and winked.

In Print

After we ate we decided to explore our new surroundings. A Dutch couple stood on the top deck. Troy and I shared their spliff and prepared for the morning adventure. Their names were Roel and Anja. We made friends, and after I made several attempts to pronounce his name, the Dutchman finally said.

"Just say Rool," he smiled. "Otherwise you will hurt your throat."

We all stood on the little terrace hidden from the road by the large leafed trees. The morning breeze felt good on the skin and the Argentine streets looked the part of post-modern colonial architecture. After a short breakfast we set off toward Elefante Blanco.

Elefante Blanco is the gambling section of town. A monstrous abandoned hospital sits in the center and looms over the darkest and dirtiest streets of the city. It comes complete with all the hedonistic experiences you can afford. On our way there, Troy reminded me.

"This is no Las Vegas. This is the barrio, the real shit. Business transactions happen behind wrought iron gates and bricked walls. If you don't know them, don't talk to them."

An hour later, it was midday, and the sun was starting to cook the inner city. The once bright white building radiated filth and grime in the sunlight. I wondered where he was and how his short adventure was going. I wondered where he might find another motor bike. I wondered about everything and anything I could to ignore my surroundings.

I was in the ghetto, or what appeared to be the edge of the ghetto. I could see two churches from the street corner I sat upon. I took long drags from my cigarettes and tried to look as uninviting as possible. Sitting like a beacon of easy pickings, I waited for Troy to return. He left me with a backpack and instructions to stay put.

It was midday and cooking hot, as I was now sitting on the steps of the old church, waiting for someone to stab me. Although I'm not a Christian, I hoped the church would provide a safe haven. A young man came walking up the street with water pouches and chicle for sale. I was thirsty but didn't have any money.

Shortly after the boy disappeared, another salesperson of sorts came up. A young woman whom I can only assume was a prostitute walked up to me and started to ask questions. I knew they were questions, but I had no idea what she was saying, nor did I have the knowledge to say anything in return.

She gestured for my cigarettes several times and the lighter in my pocket a few times more. She winked obviously while she tugged at her bright pink bra. She was wearing a fancy shirt, but it was too small and very dirty. When she sat next to me she lit her own cigarette. After a deep and audible exhalation my way, she squeezed one of her breasts. She looked at me coyly. I put my cigarette between my lips and used both hands to slide myself a little further down the step.

"No," I said with one palm out.

"Libre," she said.

Then she pointed to the small yellow brick walled house with iron bar windows. It was dark inside even with the wooden door open. I once heard a story about hookers in Thailand offering themselves for free. Not really for free, of course. When the gentlemen were inside the room and without pants they soon became distracted. This is when the family and friends would steal their valuables.

"No free lunches," the half naked British man told me one day.

"No. Gracias, pero no," I said. She looked confused for a moment then shrugged and walked away. I sat on the steps of the church for almost an hour. Finally, Troy came walking around the corner at a determined pace.

"Do you have my hat?" he asked as he approached me.

"Yea, it's right he...."

"Good." He hurried me along off the steps and I immediately picked up his long legged pace.

"Where a..." He interrupted me again.

"Shh... Just walk." I followed my orders and resumed my pace. After a few short blocks and two hard corners, Troy looked over his shoulder. He shooshed me for no reason, then stuffed a squishy paper bag in my hand.

"Put this in the backpack."

I spun the backpack off of one shoulder and then around to my front. The zipper made an ominous ZZzZZZzZZZz noise.

"Shh..." He scowled at me and put his finger over his lips like a school teacher.

"They'll be riding bikes. Did you see them?" he said with a whisper.

"Yes, they rode down the hill just after you left me on the steps."

"You didn't talk to them, did you?!" Troy's eyes grew large and his tone peculiar.

I couldn't tell if we were in trouble or he liked the danger. A few times, Troy stopped on a street corner to clamber up a brick wall or a light post. He would look around, then slide back down.

"Nothin' doin'," he said both times.

We walked through the fringes of the ghetto for several blocks without talking. Through a small, urine-drenched alley, we came onto a main thoroughfare. In front of us and across the street was a twisted brick building. Two big signs and three broken plastic chairs sat just inside. "Toros Boca's" was the name of the place. We walked in and ordered a large beer to split and a pack of cigarettes. I didn't feel as if we were far enough from danger especially since now we had drugs on us.

"We wait here for Freddy." He lit a cigarette and slouched back in his chair. Still somewhat confused but calm, I sipped my beer and then frowned.

"Wait. Don't we have what we came for? Why do we need to wait?"

"Oh. Well, I didn't actually buy anything."

"Why not? What took so long? Where did you go?"

"Oh, I went, all right," he said with a big grin.

"Well then, what's in the bag that was so important?"

"Just a treasure."

"What did you steal, Troy?" I took down the last of the beer.

"I didn't steal nothin', mate. She gave it to me."

"Who is she? And what are we even talking about? What are we doing here, Troy? Where is our fucking stuff? And why are you dragging me around the ghetto while I tote your goddamn clothes around?" I was beginning to lose my temper and my voice could be heard through the empty café.

"Take it ease, mate. Take it ease." Troy smashed out his cigarette and let out a shrill whistle. After a bit, the old woman who brought us the first beer returned with another.

"God, I hate it when you do that."

"Do what?"

"Order people around. You don't say thanks, you don't ask nicely. You're just an ass." Troy didn't like being talked to in such a manner, but I didn't care. This wasn't the first time he had dragged me somewhere unsettling. He looked down his nose at his split hairs. Between his fingertips, he tried to braid his own bangs.

"Yea, well," he shrugged. "Take 'em as they come, I guess. Don't worry about it; they're assholes too. We're all assholes in the end... get it?" He snickered and stared into the bottom of his glass.

"Fill 'er up. And what did I tell you? Don't sweat the small stuff," he said as he crossed his legs and checked the time. "Now all we do is wait for Frankie."

"I thought it was Freddy," I piped up.

"Perhaps it was... Either way. We wait."

Frustrated and hungry, we ordered a third beer and then a fourth. The midday sun that burnt my neck earlier faded into an orange hue across the dirty barrio café. Troy and I sat at that little window for three hours waiting for Frankie, or Freddy, or whoever the hell it was. I drank most of the litres and smoked a few more cigarettes before I realized the sun was almost down.

"We got fucked, mate. It's almost dark and I want outta here."

In Print

Troy shrugged and slugged down the last of his beer.

"Well, if we're going get to get rolled we might as well be a little pissed."

Outside we went into the darkened street. The eyes of street vendors set a little lower on the brow now. The indicating hand gestures from one muchacho to another made me nervous. The hairs stood on the back of my neck. I hailed two cabs; they didn't stop. Troy laughed at me and let loose another shrill whistle. One of the cabbies leaned over and flipped us off as he drove by, but the second cab stopped in traffic and popped open the door. The front door, mind you.

"Get in. Get in," the cabbie said.

Fuck that, I thought. The cabbie might take me who knows where, or maybe somebody is in the back seat and I'm about to get shivved.

"Get in," he said again, while motioning in a circle. There was only room for one. I looked at Troy. He was leaning on the light post, uninterested.

"Go, man," he said.

And I went. As I stepped off the curb, I looked back at the sidewalk in front of Freddy's. There were at least six big bodies lurking behind Troy. After jumping into the cab I looked in the back seat to reveal my possible murderer. It was a young man in a baseball uniform and an older, heavyset woman, eyes closed and snoring.

"Las Penitas, please?" I asked. The cabbie looked through his rear mirror and didn't reply until he was back in traffic.

"Ayee, man, dat is far. We will go, I need petrol. It is 500 to go to Penitas, amigo." I pulled out my wallet and showed him I had only 280.

"Oh man," he said. "Ok, for you, Gringo. You should no be out here like dis. We will go to Penitas."

He whipped the little taxi through traffic and across two lanes. We bounced over the curb straight into the smallest petrol station you have ever seen. The little green gasoline pump was just large enough for two motorbikes... maybe. Or this little Hyundai as long as two of the wheels where in the station and two were in the street.

This also meant the passenger in the front—me—was now facing oncoming traffic. Bearing down on me were a dozen bright, swerving lights. As I sat there with my eyes wide and my back glued to the seat, the lights grew bigger and bigger. Then I heard a screeching sound as one of the lights stopped in front of the cab.

The bright light flickered, then a small orange light blinked. The cabbie slid in.

"Ok, we go."

He started the car with a screwdriver. Grinding the gears into reverse, he executed a speedy j-turn and blended the cab with the exodus of traffic. Toward the city we went. Back to the safety of my little bunk. The young man and the older woman departed somewhere in the dark at a dirt road that led into the jungle. I let out a sigh of relief as the lights turned into a dull orange and faded away far behind me. The ride took an extra 30 minutes because the cabbie's little car only had three of its five original gears.

Nonetheless, it got me back to my friends safe and sound. When I arrived, the sun was down and we were still without our complete package. I headed back to the beach to meet up with our group. The Dutch couple greeted me when I hopped out of the cab. Noticing Troy's fancy new backpack in my hands, Roel said,

"Lekker. You need a bag for the party favors?" I looked at him and his beer, which still had frost on it.

"Yea, can I have a bit of that?"

"We brought you one," said Anja, then she reached behind herself and returned her empty hand with a cold beer.

"I was holding it with my ass. Is that how you say it in America?"

I couldn't help but laugh as I cracked the can.

"No, Anja," I smiled. We all laughed.

"Can we get some food now?" I pleaded to my friends like a hungry child.

"Yes, how was the journey?" asked Roel.

"Well, I got the part of the package...But now I'm on the hook for the party favors, y'know? I'm a little salty about it."

"What does 'on the hook' mean?" asked Roel. Anja answered for me.

"It means he owes us the money back."

When I got back to the hostel I found Frankie. Frankie found Troy and they had been soaking up party favors for an hour now. I was relieved to know Troy was here. There was no telling how he got here so fast. But I didn't care. I gave the backpack to Troy.

"Roll me one. I deserve it," he chuckled.

"Wish I could, mate. But Frankie's got the goods."

"Then what's in the bag?"

"Look for yourself."

I shoved my hand in the backpack and found the paper bag. Dropping the backpack on the floor, I stood in the common room of the hostel. Everyone watched me find a pair of used, wet, pink panties in the paper bag. Most likely from the girl in the ghetto.

I looked at Troy and he looked back at me. He mused like a coy friend who just used me as a decoy for the BMX gangsters while he screwed some hooker in an alley. I was not amused and now I would be stranded here with nobody but a drug dealer and one asshole of a friend. Sitting on the makeshift bench, I took a deep breath and clasped my hands.

In Print

In a short time, Anja brought me a bowl of hot Ramen with eggs and extra vegetables seasoned with a dash of hot sauce.

"That was brave to do that," she said. Roel leaned toward me with a cold beer.

"I think your friend plays jokes on you. Frankie has party favors."

Troy and Frankie sat several paces off, lounging in the bamboo chairs. They were pie-faced and elevated, I ignored them. The plastic soup bowl felt warm in my hands and my stomach was growling. I ate the soup with a clean metal spoon, then I drank, and drank another before a fireside nap. Someone turned the music up and the party began anew. I sat up from the couch.

"Whew! Ok, I'm back," I said.

"Of course he's back. You can't kill this guy," said Troy, looking over my shoulders.

"Lekker!" said Roel in his booming voice. "He has returned from dead."

Chapter 5

One Morning

A week later I was on a mission to find Troy. He, as usual, left me a note in the night. I finally found him passed out in a hammock beneath a large shade tree.

Typical Troy, I thought.

In the Arboles hostel, I showered, then swapped some clothes from his backpack. I was hungry and irritated it took so long to find him. The giant green wall and massive white sign reading "Arboles" should have given this location away.

Just on the edge of downtown, this hostel keeps a packed house. Arboles is owned by an Israeli super traveler and ecoactivist. Arboles is a self sustaining, eco-friendly hostel that operates entirely nonprofit. Employees are volunteers and tour guides for children in the community. The drive behind the hostel is educating young people about ecological consciousness.

The community supports Arboles and encourages conscious health practices in the youth. The dining and reading area is in a butterfly garden. Throughout the day, two dozen eight-year-olds shout their language lessons while the backpackers sip coffee and juice. I finally figured out where Troy had been.

A middle-aged Chinese woman painted heavily in tattoos walked past me with two cups of tea. She walked out onto the patio and set them beside the sleeping Troy. Gracefully, she turned and sat on the edge of the hammock to curl her tiny frame into the arms and legs of the big tall Canuck. He picked his head up only for a moment then saluted me with two fingers as she settled into his arms. They both slept into the afternoon. It's a shame that tea went cold. It smelled quite nice.

As I was waiting for Troy to roust, I ran across a familiar hat. It was woodland camouflage and the logo was that of a bull elk. The bull elk was stitched with jagged little white lines on the side of the canvas baseball cap. I knew that logo from a sporting goods store in Alberta, Canada.

The man wearing the hat was a young man with a short and crisp strawberry blonde beard. He had gentle brown eyes and a pudgy face. It looked as if one of his ears had been clipped. It was an inch shorter, with a straight line scar across the top. His name was George and he was from New York, New York. He made it a point to pronounce the second New

York with a dash of emphasis. I remembered back to my days in Canada.

In the fall, the ranchers would sit around the table sharing jugs of beer. They could talk about killing animals for hours. They were incredible stories. Some of them anyway. George needed a friend and I needed to hear a good ol' hunting story. I approached him.

"Need some help with that map?"

"Nah," he said to me. "Do you know where I can get a goddamn hamburger around here?"

I chuckled and remembered my frustrations in Chile.

"There are no hamburgers like you're looking for. I'd suggest the empanadas. They're like hot pockets, but your granny made 'em with real butter."

His eyes lit up. I continued.

"Tell you what, I'll buy you a beer if you can tell me a hunting story."

"Deal," he said. "Lead the way."

We shook hands then walked abreast toward the center of town. A small villa tucked behind the bus station served empanadas all day. Jamon y queso, pepperoni, and vegetariano were the steady favorites. The dark little diner also served beer in a litre bottle with two small cups.

Even if you were drinking alone you would get two small cups with a litre of beer. The Argentines look down upon drinking alone. Even the appearance of it. George and I sat down and swatted the afternoon flies off the table.

The woman who ran the restaurant remembered me and she had taken interest in teaching me Spanish. I had a suspicion she was trying to set me up with her daughter as well. The girl who often greeted the tourists was pretty, but far too young. When the mother approached our table she spoke slowly with a big smile.

"Hola, chicos." She looked at me and placed one hand on the back of my neck. Then spoke again, almost patronizing.

"Y quien es?" She asked me while opening a palm toward George. In the past, I had tried to weasel out of speaking Spanish by dent of ignorance. Yet, she was relentless in the most annoying and adorable kind of way. I replied.

"El es George, in Ingles. En español, el es Jorge."

"Genial!" She exclaimed then placed both palms on her collar bones.

"Bienvenido a mi casa. Tienes hambre?" She rubbed her belly and looked directly at George.

"Si, ambos," I said to her. Before she could speak slowly again, I made a big circular shape with my arms. "El plato grande. Please?"

"No," she said with her hand out. "Eso es no correcto. Como se dice?"

I sighed in an exaggerated way while George looked at his fingernails.

"Por favor," I said. She said nothing but kept her hand out. Then I winked at her. "Mi linda?"

She smirked then blushed a little. With one hand on her hip, she smiled.

"Todo bien," she said, then walked off down through the maze of wooden chairs.

"Enjoy the beer," I said to George.

"Why's that?" he asked.

"It's cold. Many of the Argentines are like the British and the Germans. They like their beer midday warm. This place has the coldest beer in town. And the food is cheap."

"I like the sound of that," George said before he slugged down the first small glass of Quilmes. I poured another round for us both and waited.

"Now. Let's get to the one that got away." He smiled a happy smile and was happy to have a friend.

• • •

Two months prior.

At 3.30am, George wrote his plan on a small yellow ledger. He left it on the family dining table held down by a stylish coffee mug that read:

"Xavier school of business"

- ✓ Get to Granddads
- ✓ Hunt for two days
- ✓ Come home via route 21
- ✓ Make love to my adorable loving and patient wife

As he drove into the early morning he remembered writing the note. He was very thankful to have a woman like that. She was the best thing that ever happened to him. This whole crazy adventure was her idea. From the highway he could see the big green signs.

EXIT 97 north to Pennsylvania.

"Almost there," he said to himself.

Upon the sunrise, he awoke in his car, one mile west of County Road 26. The windshield froze over night. Last night's coffee was frozen, his fingers were frozen, everything was frozen.

From inside his car he checked his platinum wrist watch. The sun would be rising soon. He wrestled himself around the inside of his economy car in search of his hunting clothes. He did not want to be outside until he had on all seven layers. The thermometer read 14 degrees Fahrenheit. Once he had his clothes on and his boots, he ventured outside to open the trunk of his sedan. Granddad's cabin was 1.4 miles into the woods. He hadn't been here in years, but he would always remember the trails behind the homestead.

That night he parked his car by the old barn at the bottom of the property. He didn't have a truck or a horse like his uncles. He only had his reliable Japanese engineered Honda Accord. George looked at the hillside for several minutes. He hadn't been here in a long time, but it was his time to sit in the tree. Just like his uncles and his brothers. They were all gone now, back to their lives in other cities. Hunting season would last for two more days. He waited for this day his entire life. No one could stop him this time.

Luck was with him that afternoon as he sat in Granddad's tree, but he came to full draw too soon. The motion in the woods alerted the wary whitetail bucks to something nearby. The wind was in George's favor and the bucks couldn't see him, but somehow, they knew.

Ever slow, the bucks walked through the bushes, one silent step at a time. They both lowered their chin low to the ground and slipped quietly through the soft bushes. From time to time they would freeze and sniff the air. The shadowy ghosts framed with white inner legs would disappear when they stood still.

George sat perched in his tree. Unaware of the constant pull of a bow string, he stood steady and held the arrow fletchings close against his cheek. He had never hunted before. He was on the family ranch and hunting was part of the tradition. A rite of passage.

The bucks always walked this direction late in the morning. He remembered Granddad telling him as a boy. A small, nondescript brown bird flew into the branches near his tree. The bird fluttered its wings for a second then, branch by branch, it hopped closer to George.

"Why is this bird looking at me?" George said to himself. The bucks were still moving toward him and George was beginning to tremble. He could feel the cold bow string digging into his fingertips. His left arm was holding the bow in his grip, his shoulder was beginning to ache. Big pillows of steam boiled from his nose. His mouth was dry and he gasped for a breath.

I can't shoot now, he thought.

It's no good. Wait. He reminded himself. *Just wait. Almost... just wait.* One of the bucks finally stepped into the small opening George had been watching all morning. It was a nice buck, not huge, but one that Granddad would be proud of. George looked down the wobbling arrow and gasped.

FZING!

The arrow came off the bow at an amazing speed and the string painfully smacked his arm. George was startled.

Whack!

In Print

The arrow found a home. George missed the buck by at least three feet. The arrow was now sunk in the roots of a pine tree. Both bucks turned from their crouch and bolted hard back into the forest. The sounds of their hooves cracking through the tree limbs was exhilarating. George took a deep breath.

"Wow," he said. "Holy fucking wow!"

The bucks were now gone and George began to feel an incredible rush. A sensation he'd never felt before. His shoulders didn't hurt any longer, his hands were hot, and he was short of breath. The hairs on his neck stood straight up and he felt the incredible urge to jump. But, he couldn't jump. He was sitting on a small 3x3 wooden platform in the snowy woods of Pennsylvania. The glowing feeling in his stomach was emanating.

He looked for the bird for a moment. It was gone. He slung the old bow over his shoulder and climbed down from the tree stand. Once his feet were on solid ground, he jumped. It was now midday.

The executive businessman from New York, New York sat at the base of the patriarch tree. Here, he ate a small lunch. Warm soup from a thermos and a cold cheese sandwich his wife made. When he opened the wax paper lunch, he found a note from her. It read:

I love you. I am proud of you.

He was so happy he was shivering; he couldn't explain it. There was no one to explain it to anyway. He looked around the forest and admired the autumn trees. After a calming breath, two large billows of steam came from his nostrils. The mayonnaise and cold cheese stuck to his teeth. He spoke aloud to himself.

"The oak tree is the most beautiful tree, I think."

Then he sipped down the rest of his soup and plopped the bread crumbs into his mouth. As he rose, he put two hands on the oak tree where he was sitting. He looked at the tree, then hugged it and kissed it.

"I'll be back, oak tree." George picked up his gear and adjusted his hat. Then he walked 1.4 miles back to his frozen little car.

• • •

"Great story," I said. "Bravo."

"I'll go back next year," he said with a squint in one eye. "I've got a plan this time."

"What's the plan?" I asked.

"Practice," he said. We both laughed.

"Good plan," I said. We shared another litre of Quilmes and talked about the big city. He wasn't too fond of the beer, but it did go well with hot butter and cheese.

Chapter 6

Fuego pit

"Pssst. Hey. Hey." Troy woke me up in the middle of the night. I was on the top bunk; his face was inches from my face.

"We gotta go...pack your shit." I checked my watch. It was 2.15am.

"Wha...why.....whe..."

I struggled to get my head on straight, still drunk and hungover from last night's party. I didn't want to go anywhere, nor did I want to move. But, I did it anyway. I crawled out of my hostel bed and smoked a cigarette on the balcony. The brisk early morning air felt good on my skin. Except my legs—I think the poisons from the night before were leaking down the inside of my thigh. Troy poked his head out from the bathroom while he brushed his teeth.

"Wherbrhd phakting duh bussfh."

"No," I said.

"Yesfh."

I did not like the idea of a bus, especially not with the revenge still reaping its spoils from my intestines. I shoved six aspirina fuertes down my throat and drank the last of the box wine. Soon after boarding "duh bussfh," I passed out.

The journey took several hours. I woke to see the white lines of the highway zipping past while Troy sat comfortably next to me, allegedly reading the *Gringo Gazette*, in the dark. I was incapable of speech due to the mixture of dehydration, cheap wine, and sleeping pills. Troy leaned into me and whispered,

"Sleep now, mate, tomorrow we will meet the Mother of all rocks."

Upon sunrise, I awoke in an old yellow school bus. Troy had both of our packs out of the rafters and sitting upright in the aisle. I could see his excitement growing with the onset of the sunrise. Barely awake and wildly trusting my friend I hoisted my pack and jumped out the back of the bus.

"Where are we, Troy?" I asked.

Troy smiled and began to wrap a bandanna around his head. He paused for a moment then smiled once more. We stood on the edge of a washboard highway that held the ever present smell of diesel and liquid soap. On one side of the highway was a ditch, no different from any other roadside ditch. Beyond that stood a long and ominous block wall. It was the exterior wall of a penitentiary, complete with many years of graffiti and barbed wire looped on the top. Troy pointed at the prison wall.

"That is their life. This is your life."

He held a perfectly round clay ball in front of me, then turned and threw it over the prison wall. In the morning sun on the roadside, we stood until one, two, three cars went by. On the other side of the road sat a typical fuel station. Behind it was a small wooden arbor with a tiled sign that read, "Fuego Negro."

Troy cinched his pack down and checked his hair. He looked back at me and pointed up the black stone mountain.

"We're going up there. Settle in."

And settle in I did. I followed him up a dark ridge-line for hours, listening to him yammer on about a rock in the carapace; a heart shaped stone in the foliage and a bush under the light somewhere near the canyon de muertos. He never found any of the cryptic things he looked for. Years earlier I stopped asking about them.

After a full morning of uphill climbing we finally reached the saddle. There he stood for several minutes looking at the mountain before us. It was boiling smoke and the rumor is you can see lava in the pit, if you're brave enough to look over the edge. Arriving at our first destination, Troy looked at his watch and then at the sun.

"We stay here. Fetch firewood."

"Fuck you," I said. "You fetch."

He looked at me and corrected himself.

"We will fetch firewood, together. Let's go, it will be dark soon."

We slept by a healthy fire in the sand beside a buttress root. We didn't speak over dinner, nor did we share the cooking and cleaning. We both sat in silence except for the rustle in a sleeping bag or maybe the lighting of another cigarette. In the early morning, we reenacted our old ritual. Someone builds a fire and rolls two smokes, the next one up gathers water and repacks the food stuffs. We had done this so many times together there was no need to talk.

Once the essentials were stored and the bags were packed, we hid them behind a tree. We tightened our shoes and set out to crawl up the sharp boulders on the way to the gaping mouth of the mountain. The distance to the rim was a mere 10 kilometers, and a 1200 foot gain. As we climbed, it sounded as if giant winged beasts were frolicking in the pit. Great swooping sounds drenched in hot air would circulate through the sky. Occasional plumes of sulfurous smoke would lift and swirl above the edge. It felt as if every stone dislodged by my foot was met with a similar groaning and vibration from the mountain. I was excited to see Earth's gateway into Dante's backyard.

An hour of climbing the sharp shards and rigid boulders left Troy and me scratched and bloodied. We continued to climb and continued to bleed our way up. At the crest, we encountered an awesome sight. A scene accompanied by an inescapable smell of earthly bowels.

Within moments Troy disrobed and knelt naked at the mouth of the pit to meditate. Meanwhile, I sat off to the side on the most comfortable of the jagged rocks, smoking a cigarette and massaging my legs. The view was reminiscent of an old black and white dinosaur film. Sweeping pockets of loose and jagged rocks scattered everywhere. Sweeping clouds drifted in tendrils around the mouth of the pit.

Only a few narrow trails existed through the imposing boulders. The grade of the mountain pulled the stones and boulders downward, constantly downward. I sat alongside the gaping hole and considered what it would be like. For only a moment. But, I considered it. As much as anyone would, I suppose. What it might feel like to fall into the bellowing chasm that is the earth's belly. If there were ever to be an eternal sacrifice, now would be the time...But I struck the idea from my mind and simply tossed a small stone into the glow.

The cigarette tasted awful. The sulfur and stench in the air burnt my throat and the jagged rocks were unrelenting on my skin. A few moments later Troy returned from the pit. He dressed and donned his sunglasses then confidently walked straight off the mountain. The only detours he took were quick steps around the boulders, which were far too big to climb over. Other than those few boulders, Troy walked in as straight a line as one can back toward our small camp. I scrambled down the hill to catch up with him. With little hesitation we exited the mountain at a rapid pace and hopped the first bus back to the city.

As we boarded the bus two small cockroaches scattered from the base of the door and dropped off into the road. We took our seats and stored our packs in the upper bunk. Troy didn't speak on the ride back, nor did I.

He often did this, a vague and extraneous journey to somewhere off the beaten track. He would remain thoughtful and solemn like this for several days sometimes.

I sat slumped into the corner of the bus with my dirty hair against the window. We were somewhere in the countryside. The road was paved and potholed for several miles then dirty and dusty for several more. The bus driver was a good driver, he seemed to be in a hurry. He would jam the groaning gears of the bus through the ruts in the road. The bus would shake violently. On the sharp right hand corners I could hear the bus cry out the sound of shearing metal. I wasn't scared for our safety as much as I was concerned for the bus. She wouldn't last long if he kept driving like this. I tried to ignore the groaning gears and the bugs at my feet.

As the night settled in, we were entertained by the local preacher. He stood in the middle of the bus holding the overhead railing with one hand and the Bible in the other. He was a heavyset man, sweating and struggling with the width of the aisle. He turned sideways to work his way up and down the rows.

The preacher was dark skinned with deep brown eyes and small hands, his blue jeans were held up by a large copper buckle. He didn't preach as much as he simply read through the book. His bumpy sermon was of Genesis and he read the story of Joseph and Jesus and Mary. Into the night the bus rambled through the small towns and pit stops. Most of the locals paid him no attention.

The old school bus now picked up farmers and uniformed students at each stop. When a new passenger claimed a seat, the preacher would waddle his way toward them to begin his sermon again. After a long stint of oily paved road we came to a large three-way intersection just on the edge of the darkness. The bus stopped in the middle of the intersection.

"Strange place to stop," I whispered to Troy. The preacher sat down, took a deep breath, and turned his attention to the rear door.

"Looks like we'll get a show tonight," Troy whispered to me.

Soon after, the back door flew open and a uniformed family began entering through the back of the bus. The mother entered first. She carried a large platter of fried meat wrapped in plastic.

"Dos pesos. Pollo. Tres pesos. Res y carne. Muy fresco."

It was late in the evening and only a few passengers bought the offerings. Behind the mother was her daughter, dressed identical: a doily slipcover with a woolen tunic and a feathered beret clip. It looked to be Mayan, Catholic, and all handmade. The young woman was next; she took her turn and said in a sharp nasal voice,

"Jugos. Piñas. Plátanos. Cinco pesos. Jugos. Piñas. Platanos. Cinco pesos. Jugos. Piñas. Plátanos. Cinco pesos."

The rest of the family came on board now, the father in the back and his two boys standing in front of him. They sang together as the first boy walked down the aisle. The boy in the front, the shortest of the three, was about 10 years old. Around both of his arms were long coils of red licorice, several meters of it all in one strand with a clear plastic coating. Of the five, he was the least happy. He sang in a droning voice,

"Dulces lejos, tres pesos," he sighed. "Dulces y mas, tres pesos."

His older brother stood close behind him and pushed him in the back. The older boy needed more space. The younger brother sulked down the aisle until he met up with his sister and mother at the driver's booth. No one bought licorice from the boy, except the driver. He was flush with cash and coin and he ordered several of each offering. What he did not finish right then he placed in a small plastic crate behind the driver's seat.

The older brother was still in the rear of the bus. He now lifted an orange plastic bucket with steam spilling out from an aluminum foil lid. He sang with bravado and used his long wooden ladle like a conductor in an opera. While he sang, his father plucked a small guitar with one hand and collected money with the other.

"Ssssssooopa caliente. Mi amooooor caliente. Y la corazón fue a la piemonteee..."

Step by step, the father and son doled out styrofoam bowls and plastic spoons to those who ordered. I wasn't hungry earlier, but the smell of hot food wafting past was enough to entice the belly. I reached for my wallet in the darkness. Troy looked over and put his finger over his lips and his jacket over my hands holding the wallet; he waited.

The father and son passed us and ladled out a few more servings of sopa. Then they fed the bus driver again and stepped off the bus into the darkness beyond the dirt road. Once the bus started back up and began to rumble down the road, I leaned over and whispered to Troy.

"Why couldn't I buy those?"

He whispered back, "You'll have the shits for a month. Sopa caliente is simmering hot sauce made from pond water."

"That sounds terrible."

"It is. I didn't lose three stone for the fun of it. There is a village up ahead a few miles. We'll get off there and eat in the cantina. The owner has a small hostel in the back."

Troy, like always, was right. After a few more long miles down the road the bus pulled into a wide open dirt field. Opposite the road sat a long wooden building with a low pine shake roof and dozens of windows. From outside you could see into the diner. The rustic building held several tables with long white cloths draped over them. A large room off to the side with a brick chimney stack poured light blue smoke into the night sky. I liked this place already. We exited the bus and walked across the road and into the well lit cantina.

It was 9.30 in the evening now and there appeared to be only one person inside. The door was heavy but swung smooth. The floorboards creaked under our weight. The smell of fresh coffee drifted through the quiet café. A woman stood up from the rocking chair near the stove and wiped her hands on her apron.

"Buenas, chicos. Me nombre, Elsa."

"Buenas," we both said.

"Scott y Troy," I said.

Elsa stuck her hand out as if to greet us, then pulled it back. She looked us up and down for a second; we were still bloody and very dirty. She leaned on one of the dining chairs and pointed at us with a frown.

"Corredores?"

"No," said Troy, "subimos la montana."

"Ah," she said and relaxed a little.

"Bien, Bien. Sientate, sientate. Ustedes mira tienen hambre."

In unison we said, "Si."

She was happy to have visitors and eager to cook. She stood at the head of the long table. Her apron was simple, her dress appeared old fashioned and stylish. She took a deep breath and then said in English.

"I try en English." She paused, then took another breath and raised her hands as if she had just invited us to a Grand Ball.

"For dinner, chicos, we have hamn, ecks, ensalad, an potahtes." She paused again then opened her eyes and looked at us with a smile. "Yes? Is right?!"

"Yes, absolutely," Troy said with a single thumb up.

She was giddy at her success. Elsa clapped her hands and jumped. Troy and I settled into the comfortable dining chairs and ate a warm dinner soon after that. Elsa shared a large bottle of wine with us and we all talked in English and Spanish as best we could. After an hour and many laughs, a middle-aged couple came in. They looked to be cold and well overdressed for the season.

As the large wooden door swung closed I noticed a black sedan sat in the parking lot, dripping fluids. The couple both wore large leather hats and stropping boots. Their clothes matched, blue jeans and a light pink shirt that read, "Unbelizable." His boots appeared well worn and heavy. Her boots looked newly scuffed and stiff. The woman was tall and pale, sickly pale almost. Her hair was long and black and she wore a silver necklace very close to her Adam's apple. The man beside her removed his leather cap and asked Elsa.

"Parlez-vous?"

"Oi, Oi!" she exclaimed with merriment and stood up to greet them.

"Frances solo?"

"Oi," said the French woman.

Elsa clapped once and turned toward the kitchen. On her way she stopped and pointed at the French couple. "Vegetarianos?" she asked.

"No," said the man.

"Oi," said the woman.

"I am." She tapped her heel on the floor.

They were still standing inside the doorway. Elsa was in mid stride. Then she got an idea. Her wine drunk smile took over her face.

"Pan!" she said loudly.

"Sit, sit. I can fix. I can fix." Elsa disappeared into her kitchen.

In Print

The French-speaking couple came and sat at the table across from Troy and myself. It was obvious they were not interested in making friends. They appeared to be hungry and road weary. They did not wear wedding rings, but they did sit close to each other. Oddly, they never touched, nor did they look at each other. Something was amiss.

Troy picked up the bottle of wine and offered it to the couple. There wasn't much left, just enough for two glasses. There were only three glasses on the table. The one for Elsa was half full, while Troy's and mine both sat empty and greasy. The Swiss man removed his gloves and reached across the table to clutch the bottle. He spoke softly and winked at Troy.

"Merci." The man drank two big gulps straight from the bottle. He handed it to the woman and she swallowed the rest.

"Merci," said the woman quietly.

Troy, fed and full of wine, sat relaxed with a hand resting comfortably on his belly. He looked at them and smiled.

"Any English?" he asked. The woman replied.

"We have some English. It is a boring and dumb language."

She winced at her own tone and then apologized with her lips. She looked downward, solemn, and only at the tablecloth. Her posture was still slumped into her expensive clothes and I had yet to see her smile.

"Please forgive my fraulein. She is delicate and a beautiful Québécoise princess," he sighed, and looked over at her.

"Alas, today she saw a thing she never saw."

"Terrible," she said, still looking down.

"Men are such foul." she added.

"Alas," the Swiss man said again. "It is truth. But, it was right to do. I stand by it." The Québécoise woman said nothing and closed her eyes; a tear began to well.

"Well, shit. I'm intrigued," said Troy.

"Do tell."

"We were driving on the roadway nearest Leon."

"Stop," said the French Canadian woman. "Not again, tabernac."

He paused and looked with one eye through the wine bottle for any remnants.

"Yes, yes, fraulein is right. After we eat, then I will tell the men. Over cigars men, yes, perhaps then." I burped after the Swiss man spoke. Before I could apologize, the Québécoise woman stood up.

"Les hommes dégoûtants." She placed her chair back against the table and walked into the kitchen where Elsa was cooking.

"Now. Perhaps?" asked Troy.

"No. Later. It is a story full of maladies."

In Print

We shared small talk and after a while the ladies returned to the table with three plates. Turns out he is a Swiss prince and she a débutante from Montréal. They met on a cruise ship off the coast of Portugal three months prior. The couple ate, and Elsa ate again. Troy and I excused ourselves for the time being. There was only one shower in the hostel and the hot water tank was heated by the kitchen stove. Now was the time to take a shower. Out the back of the cantina was a long wooden strutted hallway that led to the adobe barracks.

"Only the one shower," said Troy. He took off jogging down the hallway with his backpack in tow. We chased each other like school boys down the hallway.

"I'm going first," I shouted at him.

"Not even maybe," he shouted back. I caught up to him about half way down. I was running as fast as I could, and he was just at arm's reach. Then, in mid sprint, he dropped his backpack under my feet. I tripped and stumbled to the ground.

"You're gonna die, puke fuck," I said.

The chase was on. I unbuckled my backpack and took off from the ground like a track star. When I caught up to him I tackled him into the grass near the front door of the barracks door. We wrestled for several minutes until he pinned my arm to the ground and put me in a choke hold. After a quick flex in victory he released me and helped me stand.

"Dammit. I am going to beat you one day."

"Doubtful," he said with a smile. After both of us bathed and re-bandaged ourselves, we sat on the patio of our newest hostel.

La Buena Onda

The stars were out and Troy again had the look of deep contemplation. It was a nice place for contemplating. The growing expanse of high desert and two darkened ridge tops held up the last of the sunlight. Troy's brow furrowed underneath his blond locks.

I asked him, "What did you learn up there?"

He sat peaceful for a moment then pulled his long hair back. He took a deep breath of the evening air then laced his fingers over his belt buckle.

"No matter how you cut it, mate, how you explain it, or how you believe it, we are all small. We are all somehow a part of a giant orchestra between good and evil and the void of life and death. We humans are just innocent idiot pawns, easily swayed and more often corrupted. The one we call Mother Earth is the mother of many things."

"So you're saying be good to Mother Earth?" I interrupted.

"Not at all. I'm saying, Mother Earth doesn't give a shit about you. You are living on her skin and you are somehow supposed to be here. Yet, Mother Earth has many concerns, and you, individually, are not one of them. If you or anyone had fallen into that pit, Mother Earth would keep right on cruising; no sweat off her back."

I frowned. "I don't like the sound of that," I said.

"Meh," Troy shrugged and then relocated himself to lean on the adobe fence post.

Out of the darkness came a voice.

"'Alo gentlemans." It was the Swiss man. He was alone.

"What are we doing right here?" he asked as he walked up to us.

"Looking at the stars. Talking about life. How is your lady?" Troy asked with concern.

"She did not look well," I added.

"Ah, her? Is ok, she watch me kill two baby cow today."

I grabbed my pack of cigarettes and offered one to him.

"Sounds like story time to me," I said.

"Oh no. Cigarettes are filth. Here. I bring cigars. From Nicaragua, very nice." He pulled a small leather pouch out of his breast pocket and then looked around. There were several chairs and padded cushions around the back patio. The Swiss man perused his options. Finally he pointed at the big red Adirondack.

"May I sit, gentlemans?" he asked.

"But of course, good sir," said an excited Troy. Troy loved story time. The Swiss man sat down and removed his hat then proceeded to open the little pouch. Inside the pouch was an ornate pair of golden scissors. He clipped the cigars and lifted them to the air.

"The smoke is for you, my brother." He lowered the cigars and lit one himself. He then handed the remaining two to me with a shiny golden pearl lighter. I lit mine and then handed Troy his.

In the growing plume of smoke, the Swiss man said, "Ok. The baby cows."

He pulled from his cigar.

"Fraulein and I were driving from Leon toward sunrise. I am a good driver, yes; it was hard to see the roadway. We hired a car with room for baggage and I am happy we had the more weights. I drive around a big corner." He made a "C" shape with his hands.

"An der is a big cow. Big mad cow. In de roadway. We were driving 80 kilometers per hour! I turned wheel hard to miss the mad cow and de front of de car hits two baby cows. Bang, bang." The Swiss man clapped his hands.

"Oh fuck," said Troy.

"Yea, yea," the Swiss man continued, with his voice rising. "I hear a POP and I feel a bump. One of the little cows flew through de air like a kick in your football. It...eh... whirl in de air 20 time. Truth."

The Swiss man was amused at the memory. He used his hands and facial expressions to describe the scene. He especially liked displaying the baby cow flipping end over end.

"An, when the baby cow hit the tarmac, it land on de face and broke all the legs. It scream and scream and the mother cow was look at my car like she want to smash us."

"What happened to the second baby cow? Was it dead?" I asked.

"Yes, much dead. It wrapped in all the parts on de carriage. Like, how you say, two snakes fighting? It was like that. The intestes were pull out and under de rearend tyres. De head and bone were stuck in de frontest wheel. I pull the cow bones out with my hands, y'know?" The Swiss man smiled nervously; he had enjoyed it.

"Gruesome," added Troy.

The Swiss man puffed from his cigar and waited impatiently.

"Then what happened?" I begged.

"Den I drove de car down the road to de cripple cow. It was bleeding from every place and screams. So, der in de road, I sat on the ribs an twist de head until. Pssshshsstcccckt."

The final sound he made was that of a bloody animal being strangled to death.

"Jumping Jesus," I said, "and your fraulein saw the whole thing?"

"De whole thing," he said with a long nod.

"See?!" Troy said, pointing at me with the cigar in his lips. "Mother Nature doesn't care about you. You never know how you're gonna go out."

"Bah," I said.

We three sat outside and split the last bottle of red wine. The chill of the evening cleared the smoke and the wine led us all to silence. The Swiss man yawned loudly.

"Chicos, buen noche. I go to my fraulein now."

We extinguished our orange embers under the night sky. As travelers do, we said our goodnights and farewells to the Swiss man. Tomorrow, we would return to the city with another story to tell.

Chapter 7

Jakob

Early the next morning we returned to civilization, but opted for a campsite near the lake. I sliced my foot open on a broken bottle near the fire ring. A triangular piece of brown glass embedded itself through the bottom of my foot. With a simple first aid kit, Troy and I removed the shard and patched the wound.

It was midday, but we were still beaten up from the trail. We ate a late lunch and bandaged the rest of our wounds. Before the sun expired we both crawled into our individual tents and fell asleep before the sunset. Tonight would not be a party night.

I awoke in the early morning feeling better. I could tell the sun was out and it was mid morning. Gingerly, I felt my throat. It was swollen and painful to touch. I swallowed four aspirina fuertes and crawled from my tent.

The camp was still, so I decided to take a walk toward the beach to test my newest wound. Short of a hundred paces from the tent my foot was in searing pain. I must have pulled off the bandages the night before. I did my best to not limp the remaining fifty paces.

In the small tiled bathroom, I leaned against the counter then stared directly into my own smudged and water stained reflection.

"What have you done to yourself, Scotty?" I inquired. After a brief staring contest, I gave in and looked down. I didn't feel like berating myself right now; maybe later.

My eyes then stared again into the stranger. In the mirror, he shrugged his shoulders, nonchalant.

"No se," he told me.

I finished brushing his teeth and began to feel the aspirina kick in. After a tepid shower and with clean skin, I hobbled back to the camp. Troy started to rustled in his tent. I cleaned my wounds again, and donned another bandage. A quick bellowing cough preceded the sound of Troy's tent zipper. It opened, and Troy was followed by a small plume of smoke.

Medicated and bandaged, we were growing eager to get on our next trail. We made quick work of the campsite and morning constitutionals. Troy strapped everything into place, then he touched his forehead, his balls, then each shoulder.

In Print

"Got everything?" I asked.

"Testicles, spectacles, wallet, and watch," he said.

Our agenda:

- ✓ Check into a city hostel.
- ✓ Store excess gear.
- ✓ Get groceries for the hike and dinner.
- ✓ Check email.
- ✓ Find the quickest way to the trail.
- ✓ Camp at Jakob.

At the bus stop Troy busied himself with his daily pull-up and push-up regimen; 100 a day was the goal. I sat on the curb with my legs crossed, stretching my stiff limbs and picking at my scabs. Once we got into town, we executed our plan.

The plan was teamwork to the hostel, drop our gear, then divide and conquer. We both agreed to be quick; we were set for a long hike and wouldn't want to be setting up camp in the dark. Troy predicted our departure from the city at 2pm.

"Bullshit. We have plenty of time," I said.

The line for the meat stand was far too long and an uphill walk from where I was standing. I headed on foot through the plaza. Earlier in the week, we had eaten at a little hole in the wall nicknamed Disco Pete's.

The inside walls were lime green and techno music was blaring. Inside Disco Pete's one guy was working the counter and dancing his ass off. Pete served lunch with a huge smile on his big white face, a spacer earring in one side, and fiery, curly hair. He didn't have a care in the world. Just serving up lunch and rockin' out.

Luck was not with me though, as the line was far too long. I settled for four milanesas that were entirely too small and far too expensive. I used the rest of the cash for a pack of cigarettes and two boxes of wine. Back at the rendezvous point, I found Troy catching a nap in the sun. I rousted him and we ate. After eating the slimy sandwiches we both began to urge the unseen bus to, "Hurry the fuck up."

The clock was ticking. After two slow ambles around the block I heard Troy's shrill whistle. We gathered for a quick powwow, and then sorted out the individual bus fare. Here she came, bus 57, ambling along the potholed road with room to spare.

"Hey Troy," I nudged him.

"Yea, Scotter?" he replied, smacking on a cheap piece of gum. I showed him my watch; it was 2pm.

"Did you do that shit on purpose?" I asked.

"Crushed it," he said.

After an hour long bus ride we exited and found a local shop owner. He was very eager to give us directions to the trail head.

"Uno, dos, tres, quatro, cinco kilometros, amigos. Buen suerte tambien."

Unfazed at the addition, we ate the last of our slimy sandwiches and struck off up the trail. We kept a brisk pace for quite some time, splitting lead as we walked. The 5k passed quickly and led us to a broken sign. We wasted little time checking our map before trekking uphill toward Refugio del Jakob.

Estimated time: 4 hours. Remaining sunlight: 3h20m.

Even with the brisk pace we still found plenty of time to admire our location. The flora in the area was quite similar to home, but the mountainscape was spectacular! Huge cliff faces and crashing waterfalls pummeled the helpless stones below.

A few birds soared in the distant deep canyons, over a lifeless granite terrain. Every once in awhile we would stop to refuel. It was usually stale crackers and some kind of fruit; the kiwis were the best. We wouldn't talk much, just idle conversation between breaths. After each break we hoisted our gear back on, picked off the new seedling stickers, then resumed the trudge.

The terrain changed at the same pace as the climb. We started in a narrow canyon with a clear blue river roaring to our left. After a small ascent, we were in what appeared to be high desert with sharp and low-lying bushes. They looked soft, while cutting to touch. Soon after we were in a deep and dark green forest but steadily climbing. The vast scene appeared to me by pure compulsion. Walking up hill and tired of staring at my shoes, I drew a long breath. My mouth was dry.

Then something dawned on me: it was now windy and there were no more shade trees. Feeling the sun on my neck I slowed a few paces then stopped on trail.

When I turned around I was rewarded with the view I had only imagined. Now, looking through the center of a canyon that reached as high as the snow capped mountains, the clouds ran away from me in a smooth arch toward the sea. The sky was an ever changing shade of blue and red extending up from the horizon. It was beautiful. The sun was setting and I could feel the burden of time pulling at me. I waited only a few minutes for Troy. We shared some water and stepped back onto the path, aiming to pick up lost ground.

After a distant rumble of thunder we kicked our weary legs into high gear. Time was of the essence, conversation now minimal and effort maximal. After an hour of straight climbing, I was the first to complain.

"How long is this climb?" I said, bent over my leathery legs. My calves were on fire and it was too steep to walk on my heels. My heart pounded and my lungs begged for oxygen.

I was relieved when I heard Troy grunting in subtle objections to the ascent as well. He and I had both picked up walking sticks and we were definitely relying on the extra leverage.

With one final pit stop at a trailside waterfall, we saw a hand carved sign that read "1km." We looked at it, tightened our straps, then stepped back onto the trail. We held our declining pace for 36 minutes. As the sun disappeared, we scrambled up a pile of black granite boulders and out of the short twisted trees. In front of us lay a cabin, and a pristine lake with lush green meadows surrounding it. A towering rock spire loomed beside us, and a sheer slate bluff poured debris into the alpine lake. We made it. With some light to spare.

Ready to enjoy our accomplishment, I heard, "Dude...I forgot my tent poles."

Chapter 8

Waterfalling

The next morning was blissful. I changed my bandages after a swim in the frigid lake. Half naked I inspected the cabin and the refugio. Oddly, no-one was occupying the cabin. The doors were locked on all sides and showed no signs of recent life. It was well kept and a lone cow wandered the meadow carefree. It was as if life itself were on vacation. After breakfast Troy wandered off into the large rocks to look for a spring in the mud. Basking in the mid afternoon sun, I rested and sketched in my journal.

Two gals fresh off the trail approached from the east and asked if I could build them a fire. They appeared soaked from last night's rain and their matches were wet. I obliged and turned to dig in my pack for my own.

"See! I told you he would do it," said the one in the back.

I learned earlier in the year about the corruption of inner peace and how people aim to take it. I sat up straight and handed the matches to the gal in the front. Then I sat back into my comfortable slouch and sipped the wine from my titanium cup. The one in the front smiled.

"Merci," she said.

They wandered off a short distance to begin setting up their camp. It sounded as if one of them was British and the other French, they were fighting. Every once in awhile they would laugh and hug each other. After a few arguments they had everything set up and their fire was healthy.

Troy returned, his hair frazzled and his sunglasses now broken. He made no mind of them and swung merrily in his hammock. With a long smoldering smoke in his lips, he sung something in Italian.

The tall French gal was now wearing a bikini; her skin was smudged and dirty. A micro-towel slung over her shoulder tucked just beneath her tawny hair. I myself enjoyed a smoke and had been enjoying the benefits of box wine.

I was star struck. I never realized how attractive a woman with trail bruises and bleeding hairy legs could be. She approached and offered the box of matches back to me with two hands.

"Aurelie," she said.

"Scott," I said back. There was a powerful silence. Then Aurelie spoke in English.

In Print

"Eh, Scott, we are go to beach. You will come too?" she smiled.

I was unaware of any beaches in the Andes, yet I couldn't turn down an offer like that. I looked over at Troy still singing in his hammock. He had abandoned the need for a cup and was drinking the wine straight from the box. Without taking his lips from the plastic dispenser, he gave me a thumbs up and then lay back into his hammock.

•   •   •

The lake by the cabin poured out onto the rough stones of the Northern Andes. Just down the trail the mountain runoff carved an epic waterfall into the canyon. This was the place known in the backpacking world as "nudes beach."

There was, in fact, no beach, and the waterfall wasn't exactly epic. It was simply a place where trail weary hikers stop for a much needed shower and sunbathe. The waterfall was half a kilometer down a discreet trail, and could only be found by those who knew where to look.

The water had a slippery sense to it. The sun painted the ripples with green and purple rainbows. Here, the little fish nibble bits of dead flesh off your aching feet. The waterfall itself is nothing spectacular compared to other waterfalls around the world, and the pond isn't a shimmering emerald. Yet, when the dirt clings to the tree sap on your legs, and the oozing bug bites are caked with your own blood, this place is a day spa. Even though the sun was out, the water was exceptionally cold.

Like reptiles we were. We took turns sliding into the slippery water. Each of us dabbled around the aqua frio then climbed back out onto the large warm rocks to tend to our trail wounds. I liked sitting near Aurelie; she felt magnetic. After a sunny shower, Aurelie sat below me on the rocks. Her gorgeous figure and long French legs beamed against her plaid scarf. Her bikini was covered by a thin pink shawl imprinted with hibiscus flowers. Aurelie wore bent aviator glasses, and a trail-made friendship bracelet.

Jeanette, the Brit, sat in her ruffled one piece further down the rocks. She ignored us as she was embraced by the tumultuous current and the novelty of the little fish. Despite the wonderful view my stomach turned unsettled, the wound in my foot was aching. I reminded myself to enjoy the beautiful moment and plenty of fresh showers.

As the warmth of the day started to dwindle, Aurelie, Jeanette, and I finally left nudes beach. When we returned to camp Troy was asleep in his hammock and the box of wine was empty. I made a quick dinner and settled into my tent for the evening. Late in the night I heard the zipper of my tent crawl open. I figured it was Troy but instead, Aurelie crawled into the tent and cuddled up with me under the blankets. In the morning I awoke alone.

In Print

The sun had been cooking the tent for an hour or so and the rumblings of the other campers had quieted. I arose to find Troy pacing circles around the smoldering fire. The girls' camp was dismantled, they were packed and dressed. Aurelie saw me and walked straight toward me with a smile. When she was close she wrapped her arms around me and quickly let go.

"That was fun," she said. "It is shame we go different routes." She added a playful pout.

"Let's go then!" said an impatient Jeanette.

With a kiss I could taste her morning smoke and a hint of amorous excitement. But, the escapade was over. She was going one way, and I the other. There would be no prints, no tracks, no harm, no foul.

"Thanks for the company," I said.

"Thanks for holding," she said with a toothy grin.

Then she hoisted her pack and grabbed her expensive hiking poles. Once she walked out of sight I felt a powerful sadness. Albeit brief, it was an emptiness like nothing I'd felt before. I was smitten, and Troy could tell. I crawled into my hammock with a bag of wine and began to write.

• • •

In a rocking chair I rolled back and forth with ease.

When my eyes were gifted by your beautiful tease.

Who is the beautiful girl swinging just under the tree? Long hair flows and dances with her shoulders. I must know her name 'for I grow another day older. She travels with friends and speaks a tongue we don't share. But I'd give anything to hold that beautiful hair. I saw you eating breakfast. You saw me eat too. My entire day brightened. Just when I saw you. I stepped from my room as you were walking by. I stepped from my place as you were walking by. Even though I had practiced I could barely say "hi." I wish for those moments to come around once more. Until then... Farewell and safe travels, Mon petit Amour.

Chapter 9

Puss Pocket

A week went by at the Refugio. On a Tuesday I sat in the sun and examined my wounded foot. I felt around the gash with my fingertips and after a mid morning smoke, my tactile abilities were at their finest. Palpating the various swollen tissues, I assessed myself for pain. I examined each of my toes and found them to be numb but in working order. On occasion, I would look up and speak my findings to the trees as if they were my new students.

"Good news," I said. "It appears the mechanical elements of the foot are intact. This procedure should be an easy fix. Once we remove the infected tissue, this foot should be good as new in a few weeks."

The student trees smiled and two spiders began to crawl toward me. However, the infection was not good news. The puss pocket between my bones had been growing over the last few days and it was now the size of a shooter marble. Hot red streaks developed and were reaching around my foot. The harder I pushed on the puss pocket, the tighter I could feel my stomach clench. No one was around, I was hesitant to attempt a self surgery. Troy would not be back for days. He left me at the refugio while he wandered south to look for a river of monkeys.

I taught several courses in wilderness survival years back. It was obvious the infection was gravely taking foot. I lit a cigarette and struggled to remember the self surgery protocol.

I was confident I could cut my foot apart. Then squeeze out the yellow-brown fluid. Then scrape out the remaining chunks of dead flesh with my fishing pliers. I would sew all the ruptured or incised tissues back together. It was most important to maintain a close eye on my circulation with an open wound somewhere in the Andes.

I set out to begin surgery on myself with a Swiss army knife, a fishing kit, a vodka bottle, and one yoga mat. Luckily for me the knife was very sharp and relatively clean. The small vodka bottle was clean and unopened.

"Alcohol will be the best way to numb and sterilize," I told the trees.

I rolled my yoga mat into a cushion and with a deep breath spit out the cigarette. Then I laid a small microfiber towel across my lap and set up my miniature surgery table.

In Print

I faced the creek with the mountain in front of me and the fire pit behind. I pulled my wounded foot up into my lap then took a swig of vodka before pouring some onto the open wound. Sharp and gouging, it stung like a brier stem pulling through my teeth. My left eye started to twitch and the sounds in my ears began to fade. A pair of vultures cried out above me and the old trees groaned in defense. I took a deep breath and remembered to recite the words. As my eyes fluttered into the sun, I spoke.

Heal thyself Help thyself
Heal thyself Help thyself
You deserve to live.
Heal thyself Help thyself
Heal thyself Help thyself
You deserve to live.
Heal thyself Help thyself
Heal thyself Help thyself
You deserve to live.

With a quick breath I plunged the knife into the open puss wound and immediately vomited into my teeth. When the puss ejected onto my hands, I dropped the knife and my legs began to tremble.

The smell of the rotting flesh released into the air. Gritting my teeth I pulled the knife blade through the blister and into the open and red streaked rot. Following the lines of infection I made four quick cuts. When the puss pocket burst I swallowed my own tongue and screamed. The sweat and tears stung at my eyes as I pulled back the layers of flesh to expose the insects growing inside my foot. I learned later they are called "Luscilias."

Luscilias often infect cattle or other idiot animals that walk barefoot through the jungle. The pregnant females prey on open wounds by laying eggs inside the open wound. The larvae, up to 20, will grow as long as one centimeter before they squirm out from whence the mother laid. If the wound has healed over, the maggots will squirm and wriggle until the host scratches a hole through its own skin.

I held the vomit back with my sour tongue. My stomach quivered and begged to purge the rest of the toxins through my nose. Instead of succumbing to the acidic pain in my skull, I grabbed the vodka and poured it again into the open wound. Then I tried to swallow another swig myself.

Within seconds the searing pain blinded me and my head began to swirl. My legs wrenched in spasm. I could see my exposed tendons shorten and lengthen beneath my own flayed out flesh. Between the muscles and tendons were a dozen white maggots. All of them squirming and writhing in the bloody soup.

With blurry and weeping eyes I used the small fishing pliers to peel my own flesh even further. The chapped flesh between my toes tore further and fresh blood spurted from the wound. I did not notice my legs were drenched red and in my lap squirmed a dozen little maggots. I pulled the last of them out of my open foot and covered the incisions with a towel. Finally, I vomited upon my legs and passed out in the midday sun.

• • •

When my eyes opened I found myself back in dream space. I was lying on a crimson cot set among short trees beneath a sheer granite bluff. There were no sounds, but once again I could smell ash and burnt iron. Standing from the cot I found no handrails, just slightly visible trails to walk, thousands of faint footprints in the dirt. Faded tracks led everywhere in every direction. It was deathly still. As I walked on the old footprints, a path through the rocks became visible.

From the mouth of rocks the dirt path led uphill for 58 and one half steps. There I found a bridge that led me to a giant red door. As I walked toward the entrance I could see the same red door I was seeing in my dreams. It was surely the same red door. I could see it, yet I could also walk through it.

Inside the red door was a grand room with a buffalo standing in the center. A man in a suit wore no shoes and sat atop the buffalo, legs crossed. One of his arms extended straight out. He held a shiny silver platter and on it was a crystalline carafe with blood red liquid inside. The man in the suit never spoke and never took his eyes off me. I stood several feet below him; for some reason I could not speak.

From the antechamber three unique and ornate halls led away from each other. One of the hallways was dark, the other, bright and squalid like an infirmary. The one before me, and the one most inviting, had a saloon style gable door made of granite. I easily strode through the granite gateway and immersed myself in a shadowy hallway of doors.

Curiously, I pulled at the doorknobs. Some of them were round and polished; others were crude steel. Still others were barricaded and stood quiet, boarded and nailed shut.

Something in the air was putrid. The second to last door was deep in the hall where the lights would only flicker. The floor looked burnt with acid. The handle, unlike the others, seemed tarnished. The door itself looked beaten by a hammer and then burned with gasoline. I stood quietly, looking back to see if the buffalo and the stranger were still in the antechamber. They were.

Reaching for the door handle, my hand neared the latch. I could hear the sounds of a woman's voice. The pleasured sounds of a voice, the laborious sounds of another. My hand halted within a foot of the door. As I stared, I realized it looked like my old front door.

In Print

I put my ear closer and the fibers of the door began to sizzle. I could hear guttural screams and rhythmical scratching. Stepping back with frightened eyes, four giant letters began burning through the door.

XOXO began to sear and blacken into a cancerous bleeding scab. Ominous barking dogs and howling animals bellowed as I retreated from the door. Frightened, ghostly and morose, I walked backward down the hallway and out of the flickering darkness.

Chapter 10

Yo solo

As I awoke in real life I felt fear. I didn't know where I was. I was in a bamboo room on a stiff mattress soaked with brown sweat and wads of sun scorched skin.

The window shone to the east. I didn't know how I got here. When I laid eyes upon the gorgeous expanse of a Victorian mansion, I came to. In that little moment, I felt fresh minded, though my stomach hurt and my foot lay wrapped in gauze.

The room fan ground above me. I wanted to get up and fix it. I wanted to get up and go running. I wanted to smoke. I wanted, like always. A man wearing yellow sandals and a pressed lab coat sat in the corner of the room. He would gaze out the tall windows and jot on his sketch pad. I told the stranger I wanted a cigarette.

"No, you don't," he replied, sharp.

"Your body is beginning to purge itself. Be patient." He sounded to be South African.

"You have contracted a form of giardia and a blood poisoning. Quite frankly, you are lucky to be alive. And you are even more lucky you had a friend to save you. You will be here for some time. Do not be alarmed at your restraints; they are for your own protection. You will likely experience hallucinations, bad dreams, and fever."

Just then I realized both of my feet were strapped to the bed. Presumably for my own protection.

"How are you, sunshine?" Troy's powerful voice began echoing through the haze. I ignored the doctor and my restraints. Troy found me rubbing my forehead and groaning in acknowledgment that I was alive.

"I'm going to leave you here for a while, my friend." He entered the room from the sunlit balcony then firmly tapped his knuckles into my shins.

"Now, we have big plans for the New Year. Make sure you do everything the nice man tells you."

Troy smiled then flipped his hair back. He bit into a crisp apple, turned and walked out of the room. I could hear him singing as he walked down the hall. My journal lay open on the bed. Within it lay a drawing of a sailboat and a short letter.

In Print

We will meet on the eve of the Saint! La Islita de Arboles. The big green wall with fresh coffee. Bring jeans, boardies, sunnies, and rollies.

Vamos A LA PLAYA ... bitches.

-TH

I sat alone on the near balcony for some time and enjoyed the sounds of the birds and the distant pull of the ocean. I stayed in the hospitalita for several weeks. A beautiful couple took care of the place.

He was an Englishman named Digby and she, named Elodie, a French baker with the voice of a songbird. They were both musically talented and their secret healing house was to remain a secret.

Music flowed through the house along with the smell of fresh bread and laughter. They seemed to be great friends. Jauc and his Swedish wife, Zuzanna, were retired doctors, she a surgeon and he a psychologist.

The four of them, all retired professionals living on a hidden Victorian plantation. The towering white walls and hand carved mahogany doors were built by the pioneering Belgians at the turn of the century. I never learned how wounded travelers got to a place like this; oddly, I never asked.

Elodie and Zuzanna cleaned my wounds from day to day, and Digby often visited my room with the Sunday newspaper. After a few weeks, Zuzanna let me out of my leg restraint and handed me a pair of uneven crutches.

"Jauc says you need fresh air. There is a hammock and chairs on the balcony. You can put pressure on your foot, but do not stand on it."

After I was gifted my ambulatory freedom, I spent my days on a small balcony overlooking the tops of the trees. The ocean was in the far distance, and with a slight lean I could see the pier. The all important pier.

I met a Canadian journalist on that balcony named Kristof, and for a few short weeks we sat in silent writery. He had a small laptop and I had my trusty leather journal. He suffered from a broken rib and a gash across his scalp. His chest was tightly bandaged and fresh stitches oozed from his curly hair.

Despite his wounds, I could often hear his keys tick tick tick tick tick with an impulsive rhythm. We only broke the beautiful silence when one of us would roll a smoke, strike it, then share it. Occasionally, he would sit up straight and read his writing aloud. I would remain silent for a few moments and then offer a word. Sometimes he would scowl, other times smile.

In Print

· · ·

On day 24, the silence was interrupted by a squeaking window frame.

"For your guts, ol' boy." A voice peeked through the small hinged window. Digby showed me a smoldering joint and some hot tea. I responded with a nod.

"Thanks, Digby."

"De nada, the water gets everybody. You leave soon, yes?"

"Yea, I guess. As soon as I'm healthy again."

"You are close." One eye squinted as he drew the rolled smoke to exactly half, then handed the thick half to me.

" 'Ere mate, the rest is for you." His face made a freshly stoned smile and his hands raised with quotation mark fingers.

"I am working." He stood and turned toward the doorway. "Oh. You have a letter. I think it is from your friend."

- Indeed it was from Troy. His most recent letter read.

HARK! THE SOUL OF THE FOOL RESIDES IN THE WELL OF SOLITUDE! BEWARE ALL YE WHO REMAIN STATIONARY!

Hey, mate. I've been living with a Chinese shaman on the island. She sends these seeds to help you recover. We are building a hobbit hut on a dirt farm outside of town along the river. You should visit.

Sincerely,
Your Friend,

Troy

P.S. The train leaves at midnight.

. . .

I looked up from the scribbled letter. Kristof now rocked back and forth in his wooden chair pulling at this beard.

"How did you get here, Kristof?" I asked.

"I don't know," he said. "How did you get here?"

"I don't know either," I said.

The morning wore on as we both wrote upon the balcony.

"Kristof."

"Yea?"

"What were you doing before you got here?"

"I was surfing off the buena puenta. It is just beyond the jungle. On the Pacific side." He sat up for a moment and closed his eyes. "I can remember heading out on a beautiful day. The surf was shining and the sun was pure cosmic energy. I surfed for nearly an hour then I felt my heart start to pace and a growing headache. So, I laid down on my board and began to paddle back. That is the last thing I remember." She knocked the open door twice.

Zuzanna now stood behind us on the balcony with her arms folded.

"As far as I can tell, Kristof, you had a petite stroke. Then your body washed onto the reef."

She walked a few paces between us and turned to lean on the balcony wall. I was sitting in a small striped lounge chair with my crutches safely beside me. Kristof sat at his makeshift drafting table made of plywood and couch cushions. Our smoke filled the balcony. Zuzanna looked at Kristof.

"We dug several pieces of coral out of your ribs and your face. And, your skull may have cracked a little." Kristof sat quiet and absorbed the news. Zuzanna added one more thing then told him the story. "You owe your life to that young man."

"Which young man?" Kristof asked.

"You don't remember?" Zuzanna asked. Kristof sat silent.

"The young man you owe your life to. His name is Lysian. He is a thief in the village. For some reason he jumped out of his raft to swim to your rescue. That young man pulled you onto your surfboard and brought you back to the village. He stole your car, mind you, but still. You would be dead if it weren't for him."

"How do I find him?" Kristof asked.

"He is always in the village somewhere," Zuzanna replied.

"And for you," she pointed at me. "You are almost healed. Your friend carried you on his shoulders out of the refugio. I am surprised you didn't die up there. Self surgery is very dangerous. If the infection reached your heart, you would be dead."

Kristof left the next morning, unannounced, presumably healed. Even though we never spoke again I grew to miss him.

Chapter 11

Red red wine

The next morning I sat on the balcony with the Digby the Englishman. He handed me his rolling pouch and I proceeded to roll him and myself a fresh smoke. After I finished rolling we both lit our vices. He spoke while gazing into the tree tops.

"There is something for you in France. The universe is contacting you."

I sat still and let the smoke boil from my nostrils.

"Oh yea?" I said while readjusting in my chair.

"What makes you say that?"

"It is how she bloody works. When you are ready, the universe will send you a message. I think for you the message is France."

"Then why are you here, Digby?"

"I am your liaison, I suppose. I interpret the message. Like the one in your journal."

"You read my journal?" I asked.

"Mate. You slept for three days and you talk in your sleep. Take no offense. I have lived with her for 10 years."

His feet twitched on the balcony tiles during the rest of the smoke. After he pulled down the last of it, he stood up for a stretch then turned for the balcony door. From the doorway he looked back at me.

"Ami," said the Englishman.

"What?" I asked.

"When you are talking to her. At first, you say, 'ami.' Not 'amour.'" "Confused at the lesson and now stoned, I crawled into my favorite hammock.

"Ok, mate," I said.

I woke up hours later to Elodie's bony fingers in my ribs.

"Get up, Scott. We are on? It is pass five."

I was startled awake, but I knew how to pack quickly and hit the road in a daze. Always make sure of the essentials: Testicles, spectacles, wallet, and watch.

"Listo," I said. "Where do we go?"

"To the ocean, silly."

"Is the Englishman coming?"

"Digby? Oh no, he is with his boyfriend this end of week." She rolled her eyes and flipped her back.

In Print

It took but a few seconds to put together what she meant. Then I remembered the conversation with Digby. They were married, but he had a boyfriend. His boyfriend was visiting from the city and Digby wanted the house for the weekend. Elodie wanted to go to the beach.

● ● ●

When we stepped off the collectivo, we immediately bumped into an arguing couple. Canadian backpackers, discernible by the large maple leaf sewn onto their packs. I later learned they spent every day for nine months together, not a stone's throw apart at any time.

She looked a princess and he a rough type; hockey goon, no doubt. With several menacing scars and a dragon tattooed across his bicep, he was hard to miss. His hair was long and brown, ragged and wildly strewn.

"You'll never see those people again, Aymee! Ever. They live in other countries. And seriously? Would you rather be the lady who peed in the bushes? Or the tart who pissed her pants? It's your call. But, if you have to pee, then go pee in the goddamn bushes!"

"I am not going to pee in the goddamn bushes, Shane." Aymee held her legs crossed with a burlap purse clutched between her bright pink fingernails. He looked at his large wrist watch.

"The bus will be here soon."

"So?" she snapped.

Their mutual patience had run out. He turned and began walking away while continuing to talk.

"Ok, I'll be at Blue Bottle."

"I'll meet you in the city!" she shouted after he had walked a good distance. "I love you!"

"I love you too," he shouted back. Aymee looked around and cursed at the dirt. Elodie looked up at me and whispered.

"I would pee in the bushes."

"I love that," I said.

We clasped hands and laughed. From the bus stop Elodie and I hired a tuk tuk. This one was a small red cab with two plastic windows.

We traveled down the ocean road to a small villa named Todo Esperanza. It was a tourist attraction, but in a different manner. It was designed so, when you checked in, you would also mentally check out. There were many private coves and secluded trails through the ocean side foliage. We held onto the tuk tuk as it came rambling behind a plume of diesel smoke. Gazing out the dirty little acrylic window, Elodie pointed at the tide. The choppy waves were crashing red and brown. Each little tourist stop seemed amiss. It only happens a few times a year, but red tide was upon us all.

In Print

The cabbie's creaky tuk tuk bounced its way along the jungle road. The driver's name was Edward. He would occasionally pass his bottle of homebrew to the back row. I drank a few mouthfuls of orange flavored banana wine and passed on the puffs from his copper pipe. Edward ranted about gossip in the community and how he never gets a day off. He drank and drove and smoked and sang.

Elodie's sweaty skin was stuck to the dusty vinyl seats. My head bounced off the ceiling of the little tuk tuk. We rode like this for almost an hour. By the time we reached our final destination, I was half-drunk and my stomach was bitter. I needed to eat. Edward looked at me in the tiny mirror.

"How long you en Esperanza?"

"No se," I told him with an exhausted smile.

"Do you need drogas?"

"No, no. I don't need 'em."

"You will," he said. He stared at me then pulled a puff from his stubby cigar. "She will find you."

After a brief silence the cab driver looked at the sleeping Elodie on my shoulder. The tuk tuk slalomed down the dirt road while he grabbed the fake diamond crucifix hanging from the mirror. He looked at me and said.

"Dios mio, tu dama es magnifico. Will she go you in Heaven?" I nodded, but said nothing. After a while we cleared the jungle tree line. The road turned to loose sand

and now we could see the ocean. Edward glanced at me with concern.

"Joo surf man?" I nodded. "Now is no good time, man. You should no swim in waters, y'know, man?"

"Por que no?"

The cab driver lifted a limp wrist and wiggled his fingers in a sweeping motion.

"Joo know como la damas limpiar in a month, man? It's like dat, man, de uhm...deh mother ocean is clean herself. She is on period now, and she is angry jajajajjajaja."

He was still laughing at his joke when we arrived at the beach. After we paid Edward, I could see exactly what he meant. A thick layer of mucous discharge sifted across the bay. The waves pulled globs of foam and stringy remnants from the ocean floor. Crabs and various carcasses scuttled across the beach, each little scavenger unwillingly covered with slime and reeking of putrid sea flesh. Seagulls swarmed in small circles looking for something to eat. Even the hungry birds would not land near the ocean's waste.

Pigeons usually occupy the villa strip in Todo Esperanza. Today the lanes were buzzing with all the little creatures unwilling to eat the leftovers. Elodie and I walked hand in hand on the high side of the beach. The conversation strayed from the ominous water into looking for a safe haven. A kilometer or so down the beach we found the resort bar called "Blue Bottle."

In Print

Blue Bottle was owned by an Australian lady named Tanya and a local man named Luis, who owned several of the little businesses in Todo Esperanza. They were the envy of the beach. Over a few years they built a tree house palace on the edge of the Pacific.

A single stone foot path through the middle led the sun weary tourists to their drinking tables. The expanse of restaurants and bars had their own security force, with the edge of the property barricaded by a jungle made jetty and a jagged reef on the far side. There was one way in and one way out of Todo Esperanza: through the gate, and past the man in the Aussie hat. His name was Stephan, and Stephan is a German prick.

When you walk through the maze of jungle trimmed hedges, you feel as if you're walking into a miniature village. Dozens of strong palm trees decorate the landscape, and each tree housed a little human sized nest. Out of each nest comes a dumbwaiter. From the bamboo pulley you can tote your luggage, or a day's fresh water. Even room service is available from time to time.

The ocean sits just down the hill, where you can fish or kayak or lie on the small sandy beach. Countless hammocks lay tucked away in the gardened atmosphere. In the center of the village is an octagonal building partly cut away. It holds a host of guitars, djembes, and many soft chairs to lure traveling musicians and artists.

Elodie and I checked in at the octagonal hut and stored our stuff in our own little hut. We shared a spliff and a nap under a wondrous view. After we dozed she washed her face in the sink then donned her big sunglasses. She covered her curves with a light floral dress and slung a small purse across her suntanned shoulders.

"Let us eat now. I have hunger."

Elodie stayed with me for three glorious days. With the sounds of the trees, and the ocean off limits, we didn't leave our room much. It was splendid. Fresh breakfast via dumbwaiter into our private view of the jungle. When she left, she kissed my cheek and opened my journal.

"I write?" she said.

"Of course."

Just like Sira from the city, she rubbed the rolling paper along her neck and shoulders to anchor her scent into it. She wrote a number and an address on a Zig Zag then delicately placed it in a blank page seam. It was a pleasant goodbye kiss.

Elodie the songbird hitched a ride with a local couple back to the bus station and back to her life. She gave me her box of cigarettes as a "remember my byes." After a nap in a beach side hammock I settled into life on Bombero Beach.

• • •

In Print

I smoked her last Belmont on the patio of the Blue Bottle. I was thankful to have met her: long brown hair, light brown eyes, and her full figured two lung laugh. With short strolls on the beach and long kisses in the dark we enjoyed each other. But today there would be no more kisses. Today, I sat and remembered in full detail.

Her scented curves decorated with salty sandy sweaty sex. I smoked and strove to remember how she pressed her back into my chest. When she pulled her hair to the side and how she sighed when I kissed her neck. I pulled the last of the Belmont smoke down and exhaled through my nostrils. Looking over the edge of the hammock I touched the simmering ember into the standing water.

"That'll do," I said with a smile.

"Who are you talking to?" asked the Canadian man from the bus stop. He was standing behind me outside his new hostel dorm room.

"I'm talking to myself. Who are you?"

"I'm Shane. Most people call me Tennessee."

"MC. Most call me Scott. Well met." We shook hands like friends. A fisherman can spot a fisherman a mile off. He pulled up the hammock next to mine and we became the Bomberos.

"Did you by chance see if my wife got on the bus?"

"I saw her get on a bus, but I couldn't tell you which one."

"That's good enough. How long are you traveling?"

"I don't know."

"Do you have a woman?" he asked.

I looked down the long dirt road parallel to the beach. Elodie was long gone.

"Guess not," I said.

"I'll give you some free advice. When you get one. If you love her, don't spend every single day together. It causes irreparable fights."

I clinked glasses with him.

"Cheers to that, Shane."

"Do you know where I can get some drugs?" he asked.

"No," I replied. "Do you?"

The next day a small man named Diego with a large scar across his face and a clubfoot met Shane and me on the dock.

Chapter 12

Diego

Early the next morning Luis was nowhere to be found. Diego was leaving with the outgoing tide.

From our hammocks, Tennessee and I heard a distinct whistle from the dock. It sounded like the parakeets from Nicaragua.

Hhooooiit hootiitit hohot. Hhooooiit hootiitit hohot.

"Can you hear that?" I asked Shane.

"Yea."

"It sounds like a parakeet."

"Ha!" Shane laughed as he swung merrily in his hammock.

"It's one big goddamn parakeet then. Should we go look?"

"Sure. Let's adventure."

We sauntered down the beach and made our way to the dock. Halfway down the dock Diego was leaning against his rusty fishing boat, "La Inspiracion."

Diego was a man with one eye, a club foot, and seven fingers. A fisherman all his life with a large image of Christ painted on the side of his ship, Diego was stern but more importantly he was nervous; he owed Luis a favor. He looked at us, two tall white gringos, then he slapped two large kingfish onto the dock.

"Ders dems deal. Fer Luis. Wees even."

Shane and I each picked up a fish and hoisted them onto our shoulders. Kingfish are large and very slippery, but the tail is wide and rigid like many other sea fish. Both kingfish weighed about 20 pounds.

"Finito," said Shane as we walked off.

After a hundred paces Shane looked back toward La Inspiracion, then he asked me, "Does it feel like there is something in your fish?"

"Indeed it does, Shane," I said with a grin.

"What do you think might be in there? I mean, who would gut a fish then sew it back up? Seems a bit cheeky, I'd say."

"Agreed," said Shane.

"Let's set 'em down in the shade and open 'em up."

In Print

Inside the dead fish we found two black plastic waterproof boxes. Both boxes were filled with several sealed plastic bags. We took the fish to Luis and Tanya's house up the hill. Only Tanya was there. She was half dressed and very hungover.

"What do you cunts want?" she demanded.

"We have your delivery from the dock," said Shane.

"What delivery from the dock?" she said through a labored yawn.

"Diego said these fish were for you," I said, while holding the dead gutted fish out for her to take.

"I don't want those disgusting things in my house. Get out of here," Tanya snapped then closed the door.

"I'm sorry to have bothered you, ma'am. There must be a mistake," I said.

Shane smiled when we turned and walked back down the courtyard fence carrying our drugs and dead fish. Tennessee flexed one arm, then punched at the sky.

"We scored huge, mate. Y'know, I never intended to be a drug runner again, but life has a funny way of putting you in profitable places."

Chapter 13

Make some party

One of the best little beach bars inside the false town of Todo Esperanza was "El cat." The bar is small and the front door shuts early. The breakfast is hearty and included in the room price. Shane convinced me to move out of the honeymoon hut and into the dorm rooms. This would be the best place to move the products.

"You don't want to stay in that little place, man. Leave it for the newlyweds. Come stay on the hostel side. It is cheap as hell and it comes with free breakfast and tea. The pipes don't usually work and the roofs are never quite finished, but this hostel has a bright little gem." He smiled and winked. "The balcony. It sits three narrow stories above the path and it has two dorm rooms side by side. The balcony itself is long and skinny and can comfortably hold four or five. But that doesn't stop backpackers from jamming ten or more up there sometimes."

I took his advice and moved out of the little thatch honeymoon tree house and into the top story of "El cat."

From here you can see the other decaying roof tops and some volcanoes in the distance. Sometimes, you can see the volcanoes erupt while sitting eye level with the bell towers.

Breakfast was over and the seductive sun was working its magic on my pale skin. Tennessee sat oddly propped on an oddly small chair plucking an oddly small guitar. It was a tune he had been working on for some time. It involved sitting around, waitin' around, waitin' on something to do. A tune with a dozen various ways to describe our life, us, us unrequited backpackers.

On the balcony you can see three volcanoes. Two of the three erupt often enough to attract tourists to cook a marshmallow over molten lava. You can also see about two dozen abandoned buildings and decaying block walls. It wasn't only the old Catholic churches that were falling into decay.

The entire town was falling apart, but life here moved slowly and everyone seemed to be fine with it. Shane continued to pluck on his strings and I decided to roll another cannon.

One song and one joint shaped train wreck later, we smudged out the stogies and prepared for the crowd to set in.

In Print

A tall and smelly German man came up the stairs sniffing the air like a bloodhound. He spoke with terrible beer breath.

"Where can I get weed?"

We played dumb.

"I don't know, man."

"Where did you get this?" He pointed at my smoldering spliff in the ash bucket. Then he gulleted the rest of his tall can, paused, and looked at us with a grin.

"You boys want to ahhh...make some party?"

Shane screeched his palm down the guitar strings. He and I looked at each other, then the pesky German tried again.

"I know of some local girl. She is fifteen hundreds. I say ehm, five for each. Yes?" A brief moment lapsed and I exhaled.

"Are you asking us if we want to triple down on a local under-aged hooker?"

"She is 20 years and only fifteen hundreds. Is too much moneys, but she is very sex."

"Uh...no, mate," I said.

"I'm a married man," said Shane.

He shrugged and said something in German. He then took a big swig from the tall can and crushed it while flexing his arms. He looked at us, disappointed, then shrugged again before sauntering back down the stairs.

Several internationals sat at the community table that evening. The German obviously found a girl and ponied up some cash. He brought her to the dinner table and acted as if they had been together for years. He put his arm around her, and asked her questions the way an older couple checks memories with each other. He bought wine for the table and two litres of beer. Shane and I made a silent bet that her jade necklace was brand new as well. The local girl was attractive, but very quiet. When the other travelers asked her questions she would only reply with short responses and usually with her head down. She had two children and a deceased husband.

Meanwhile, the German held her hand and made jovial conversation with anyone he could. The Israeli band of brothers would have nothing to do with him. The Kiwi hippies and the rude Italian couple tolerated his banter but disregarded him as a liar. The communal meal at the table was nice, but the conversation was strange. After dinner and more wine, the German and his new girlfriend excused themselves.

The Italian girl asked after a brief silence.

"Como se dice...that was very awkward?"

Chapter 14

Bomberos

A corvid sat in my window the next morning. Perched and silent. In his beak was a crawling grub, squirming from the pinch. The bird sat calm on the sill and waited for the grub to stop squirming. After a few moments and a quick gulp the grub was gone. Puffed and ready for the rainy season, the corvid ruffled his feathers once more. Without warning, he set wing to dig out the next morsel.

I rose from my small bed and resumed my snooze in the sun shaded hammock. Shane looked at my flaccid belly swinging in the sun.

"Hell yea, brother. You've got the right idea now."

I gave him a sleepy smile and clicked my pen several times. After a week or so Shane and I were heralded as Bomberos. Inadvertently, we had developed the mocking reputation. We would walk the beach in the day and build bonfires at night. For the first two nights we had no fire, just the crashing red waves, the stars, and cheap booze. And cigarettes, of course. On the third night the sun dipped beyond the sea and the oranges and purples began their nightly dance. Across the sky the colors ran streaks of the rainbow around the will o' the whispering clouds. Shane spoke after a long silence.

"We should build a fire."

"Right now?" I said, astonished and lazily through my straw hat.

"No. Tonight. Everyone loves fire. It will bring people down to the beach. I'm sure of it. I mean, we gotta sell some of this stash, right? And we could cook those kingfish. Neither of us can put down this many party favors without melting some brain cells. It would be a shame to let those fish go to waste."

I could see his point, but unlike him I did not want more attention or more people around. I was content to sit right where I was with my copious stash of party favors. He convinced me otherwise, and over the next five nights we built a bonfire and let the people and the money come to us. He was right. The fire on the beach drew people in like moths. Young couples, older couples, singles on the prowl. All looking for a good time, and good times for any ilk could be had.

In Print

After five all nighters, we exhausted all the firewood within a half mile in both directions. The party lasted as long as we had firewood. Obviously, over a week's time we found less and less wood. After seven straight days Shane and I decided we would head for higher ground. We agreed it would be best to get rid of the rest of the stash before we walked past Stephan at the gate. He was an untrustworthy sort. By now Luis had to know where his delivery went.

Ready to go, I woke up in the morning to see the tide had brought in piles of ripe driftwood. I looked to my left to see Stephan with a cigar and a new Aussie straw hat. I looked at the sun through the palms. It was almost noon, time for a midday smoke. I checked my shorts and found a fresh pack of cigarettes and a different colored lighter. Confused, I took the bait and put a cigarette in my lips. I sat in the good hammock to watch another day pass.

"S'alright," I said to myself. "We'll have a fresh one."

"Just wait 'til we get to Colombia, mate." Tennessee tossed the little treasure chest into my hammock. I opened the chest and found a small portion of the favors remained.

"You didn't give all this away, did you?"

"Nah, mate. I got us handled. Prep us a good time and I'll show you what I've done."

So I rolled a big one and portioned out the rest. When I turned around, Shane was standing with two thick wads of euros and dollars, one in each hand. He smiled like a idiot.

"The Russians. I haven't counted it yet, but you can have either stack." Both stacks contained plenty of cash for several months of travel. I looked at them and snagged the wad with the most visible Euros.

He smiled again and said, "The Russian brothers want to be the Bomberos now. We have only a bit of work to do, and then I am off to the city to find my wife."

Rich with cash and no worries, we agreed to split the last of the treasure chest over the next day.

The next morning we rose and walked down to the water as was our ritual. Dabbling my toes in the reddish foamy water, I looked around the beach. I sighed, dismayed to see dozens of new driftwood piles. I looked down at my feet and then back up. The frothy red mucous clung to the hairs on my legs. I felt like vomiting when I thought of the slimy entrails that sifted through my toes. Shane lit a cigarette and stretched his shoulders.

"I am off to see the shaman and then the hammock festival in the jungle. You sure you don't want to come?"

"But, mate, the Bomberos have work to do." I gestured to all the firewood on the beach.

"Nah, it is time I go. You can overstay your welcome anywhere. Stephan and his hat have a bitchy way of telling you it is time to leave. Luis is pretty mad that we cooked his food and sold his drugs." He put his cigarette in his lips and flicked his long hair back.

"And besides," he added, gesturing back toward my legs, "that shit is gross."

The Bomberos stood shirtless on the open beach. Then and there we shook hands and jousted each other with locked arms.

Shane, the hockey goon, walked up the beach toward the palm trees. His red backpack sat beneath a grassy sand bank. I looked out to sifting purple waves and watched a small crab skitter across the shore. When I looked back, Shane was gone.

Chapter 15

Luis is an asshole

Alone again, I sat on the balcony of the Blue Bottle restaurant with the select company of day old coffee and a concert of waves.

I could live here, I thought.

From here I could see to the extent of the horizon and into the listing blue of foreverness. I could sort my troubles from my worries and mull over my mistakes from here. Some days, I could stand and lean into the wisdom of the ocean and some days, I would learn her language. Relinquishing my date with the sun soaked hammock, I sat at the bar instead. Alone again, it all felt like emptiness.

When I finished the coffee I pulled down the last drag of a spent indulgence then returned my gaze to the black, sound crushing waves.

From my shaded perch I could see Luis, passed out with a big belly full of foam. His legs hung twisted off the picnic table and one of his sandals dangled from his toes. Tanya lay near him, her eyes closed and her skin rippled with goosebumps. One nipple stood firm while she slowly drug her fingernails up and down her throat. Her feet twitched while she giggled and blinked at the sun. Tanya was soon coming down and Luis was throwing up.

In that moment the balcony with a view to nowhere became a platform of bodily fluids and broken glass. Puke, piss, and shame everywhere. This place was no longer paradise. The ocean now seemed a purple wall of emptiness. The sun was no longer warm on my skin; it was now a constant itch of burning flesh. The children who played on the beach, now seemed cruel and mocking. I wondered about Troy and realized I hadn't thought about him in weeks.

I decided I would walk down to the beach. Red tide had cleared and the beach again looked clean. Staring at the long waves down the beach I saw a little white puppy playing with a piece of driftwood. The puppy was carefree, no collar and an entire beach to himself. There were clean crabs to chase and flocks of standing seagulls to run through. I smiled and watched in envy. A torn sandal flipped about in the air and a forgotten towel became the puppy's matador rag.

The sun burned at my shoulders and my forehead was pounding. The coffee I brought from the lodge was bitter and unappetizing. I lit a cigarette and lowered my sunnies. The puppy worked playfully toward me and scampered up the beach with two treasures in tow, an old dirty beach towel and a chunk of a futbol. I could see from where I was it was a young pup, innocent and unafraid. No scars or marred ears, no collar and sharp little teeth. He panted and lowered his head a little before he crawled closer to me. My cigarette burned in one hand, while he sniffed at my dirty feet.

Then without prompt he circled in place and plopped down to watch the rest of the sunrise. With his trophies set at his feet he lay on the towel and looked around happily. I put out my cigarette and scratched his back with both hands.

"How about we call you Max?"

The puppy shook his head and flopped his ears back in approval. After the sun had risen and Max scampered down the beach, I mustered a small amount of motivation to do something. I hauled myself off the shaded beach and ambled down toward La Piscina.

My pack was in Fredo's basement. With little effort I found the owner of the La Piscina sitting on his very own splintered deck. His name is Fredo, and he was Luis' right hand man.

Fredo always sported thin and airy shorts, artificial boots, and often no shirt. His fashion sense came from textiles left behind by travelers. As I stepped up the last of the broken brick staircase I saluted Fredo in his new Che Guevara hat and rattlesnake boots. When he saw me he stood up, wobbled for a minute, then commanded one of his cronies to pour me some RON. I didn't need a full glass of rum, but I wasn't going to complain.

"Hey, Fredo, do you think Luis will mind if I get my gear and bail out of here tonight?"

The delayed response and stupid smile tipped me off. He was intoxicated and probably stoned too. I overheard some giggling and the snap of a beach towel inside the house. My party ended last night; Fredo's party hasn't stopped for three days.

"Do you have the cellar keys? I need..." I was cut off.

"Luis?... Bah, he is an asshole. We went to uni togeder. He will get nothing from her. Tanya is too good for him." I spoke out of turn.

"Steve wants Tanya y'know."

"Jknow man, I respect your ehm... smart. Luis knows, man, he knows. He say to me in whisper while you sit in the beach. He say, 'this hijo can make me rich again but, no, this man will no bow down to me.' "

"Yea, well, I can't fix a sinking ship," I said with a sip of good rum. I did not want to be there nor did I want to continue this conversation. Yet, my bag remained locked in the basement, and I had a big wad of Luis' money.

"Jahajahahhajah." Fredo leaned back onto his rattlesnake boots.

"You say it, man. Gracias, my friend. I am always explain things to all dem con picturas, y'know? Jaja."

With another bellow of his belly laughter he lost his balance. Luckily one of his bikini clad cronies caught him. The skinny brunette reached her hands into his pocket, giggled, then returned to the shade of the parasol. Fredo looked at me over his designer glasses.

"I know men like you." He anchored his sentiment into my chest with his pointy finger. He stuttered while spilling some spirits on me.

"I say to you...Fuck him, keep your money. I don't share my booze with gringos. Jus' doss gringos I like eeeee, and I ehm...I like dis gringo."

"I appreciate you and your...how you say...man hooed? You are terrible Spanish, dios mio, que terrible. But, you don't say; por favor por favor, gracias amigo." He waves his palms toward the sky while parroting and mocking one of the bikini clad cronies. He continued.

"I mean intellectly, o eestory o.... d'er education is bad man. But dey like it here. Dey know de game." In a similar low tone, I chuckled and took the burning spliff he offered me. Fredo continued with the loose jaw.

"Heh, see mate, I make dem buy the ice and the coke. The rum is a gift from doss guys. I spend nothing." He shrugs and spills more ron on the deck. "See? We profit. 'Ere. 'Ere," he repeated while digging in his pocket.

"You are good business for me, and buen company if you had more Spanish. I tink dat Swiss girl like you, y'know?"

He pointed his boozy finger at the tall and athletic Croatian blond sitting by the floating dance floor.

"I think I like her too, Fredo. I am looking for a lady that doesn't sleep at your house." I drew a long puff from the spliff and looked out over the ocean. For a moment Fredo sounded serene and sober.

"Cuidado, amigo. We are almost 40 years, man. You are no as old, but I think you are understand. You are good to have around. You share work," he said with a sad voice. I interrupted him.

"How much do I owe you, Fredo? Quanto quieres ... para todo?"

"Bah!" he said while swatting the air. "Dem de uh... money es no importa from you. Dees girls will stay with me for three weeks. Dats 45 time 21 time three. Per chica. And doss Russian guys are rich. We smart guys profit from each-odder. You should go wit dat Croat lady now. She want a husban' like joo man. She say to me she wants many babies."

"Don't believe 'em, Fredo," I said. With a wink, a nudge, and another spill of rum he leaned in and, for the first time, he turned off the hustle entirely. His face grew wrinkled and stricken. He pinched his burning septum and sniffed a sneaking tear. With a shaking hand, his empty RON glass dropped to the deck. Fredo didn't move. He hung his head and looked down at the broken glass. The fresh ice dripped through the boards.

"I has two girls, man, jknow? One in Frances and the other in Espana. Der mothers come tru 'ere many years ago. Mararae speak to me sometimes, Fendra won' speak to me after the prison." I was curious about the women who birthed his children, and I was curious about the prison. He didn't bring them up and I didn't press. He wept slightly before flicking his nose again and then again swallowed his pain. I relinquished the spliff back to his empty hands.

"Joo don't kno' what I am talkin'. I make paradise for dem if dey would come visit. Look, look, amigo."

He took a long step to the edge of his seaside balcony and put his arms out wide. "Joo see, man. Joo see what I mean, man. I make dis for dem. I make dis."

His hands clenched and his belly began to quiver. The large plastic sunglasses shielded his bloodshot eyes. They could not catch the tears that began to fall. He leaned over the railing for a moment then stood up straight and again dug into his pockets.

"Take dees, I don't need dem." He placed two baggies of cocaine and two blue pills in my palm. We clinked glasses. Fredo put his greasy palm on my shoulder.

"Cheers, we are the old dogs on de track, Bombero. I am sorry to see you go, but I am happy you find your way out."

As I walked down the beach I decided to abandon my big pack. Luis could have it. I had a small pack, a passport, cash, and a destination.

Back at "El cat," I left the party favors on the window sill for someone else to find. I was no saint, and I would have kept them for barter. But, I remembered a story from Kristof and the lesson that came with it.

"Never cross borders with illegal things. There are illegal things where you are going."

My small bag sat packed and I sat on the porch overlooking the ocean. It was a crisp azure blue now fading off into a dark royal purple. The gravity of the green flash pulled me to my feet.

"Sunsets are spectacular," I said out loud.

I left in the night.

Which I was prone to do.

Stay tuned for

"Islita."

About the Author

I met MC on a bus in the dark. It was a long night with moonlight scattered between the cacti. He was too tall for the seats, but he held a consistent smile. We greeted each other as travelers do and shared a small bottle of mezcal while he wrote in his journal, his feet dangled above the floor boards. We talked of our travels and he spoke fondly of his home.

He wore a mix up of dusty clothing and his trusty black beanie. I would call it a touque, but he calls it, his trusty black beanie.

When the bus stopped somewhere in the desert, MC checked his map then exited the bus with haste.

I never saw him again.

As with many wandering souls, we met for only a moment. As the bus rambled on down the Mexican highway, I saw him standing under the light post, smoking and looking happy.

Otro Viajero.

61743623R00081

Made in the USA
Lexington, KY
19 March 2017